THE SHADOW

Maurice Level (1875-1926) was a writer of fiction and drama who specialized in contes cruels which were printed regularly in *Le Journal*, *Le Monde illustré*, and other newspapers. He wrote thirteen novels and at least ten plays, most of which were performed at Le Grand Guignol, the theatre specializing in naturalistic productions which emphasized blood and gore.

MAURICE LEVEL

THE SHADOW

Translated by
BÉRENGÈRE DRILLIEN

THIS IS A SNUGGLY BOOK

This edition Copyright © 2018
by Snuggly Books.
All rights reserved.

ISBN: 978-1-943813-86-5

This translation of *L'Ombre* is an amended and somewhat revised version of that which was originally released in 1923, under the title *Those Who Return*.

THE SHADOW

I

AT three o'clock that afternoon, the heat of the sun was overpowering in the street.

Claude de Marbois came to a standstill in front of the door that made a dark cavern in the dazzling whiteness of the walls, and thought:

"Shall I go in? . . . Here's another to whom I shall have to tell my story, who will listen with half an ear, without in the least understanding what is the matter with me, and who will tell me to come back again, after giving me advice which I shall not follow . . ."

For months he had known and feared this vacillating state of mind. For a week he would be as other men, then, suddenly, doubt took hold of him. At once he lost control of his will, could not make up his mind about the most ordinary decision, and finally left everything to chance. Only a moment ago it had seemed simple and sensible to go and consult the doctor; now it appeared complicated and useless. However, as the heat made his temples throb, the cool archway and freshly washed cobblestones tempted him. He crossed the threshold and inquired for Doctor Charlier.

The drawing-room into which he was shown was huge, luxurious, and depressing. Loose covers, bordered with red, enveloped the seats. The daylight, filtering through the shutters and closed red curtains, darkened about the wainscoting; the beadwork and caryatides of a Buhl cabinet gleamed in the corner; a crystal chandelier, veiled in net, shook and tinkled when a carriage passed in the street.

On his right, a man and woman were talking in whispers, between them was seated a little girl.

She had a pale face and fair hair, glassy eyes, a thin-lipped mouth, which opened to show teeth with a gap between them. Now and then the mother smoothed the child's face with her fingers and when she did this, the father looked at the grief-stricken woman and the idiot child with an expression that was almost that of shame.

On his left a young man was seated on the edge of an armchair. He was gesticulating wildly, his hands with their twisted wrists and crooked fingers beat the air unceasingly, his shoulders jerking up and down at the same time, following the movement of his hands. Behind him, an old woman, probably a nurse-housekeeper, was dozing.

When the portière was drawn aside, Claude saw a hand holding it back. The first group of people stood up. Then he saw that the little girl was paralyzed, and he began to turn over the magazines scattered about the table, with one ear straining toward the mystery of the adjoining room. After a short time, the door opened again and the wildly-gesticulating man crossed the room with the help of the old woman, throwing his arms about, limping, lifting his feet like a prancing horse, and uttering little cries.

As soon as he was alone, Claude began to walk up and down the room, stopping to glance at a knick-knack, to pick it up, and put it down again.

When he had almost made up his mind to go, his turn came. There was the same shaded light and the same coolness in the doctor's room as in the drawing-room. But his attention was riveted on the man whose fame had attracted him there, and to whom he was going to tell his trouble, so that he had no time to notice the surroundings particularly.

"Monsieur," said he, as he seated himself, "it is not my intention to set you a medical problem. I should like to say that I understand my case as well, better even, than any physician you care to name . . ."

And as the doctor slightly shrugged his shoulders, he corrected himself with a constrained smile:

". . . or, at any rate, the symptoms . . . I eat well, and usually sleep well . . . There is nothing wrong either with my digestion or my heart. And yet, I feel that I am ill. I feel it, as you may feel a dog lying stretched across your bed, a good, obedient dog who does not get in your way, but whose presence you realize because of the warmth and gentle breathing. My malady is here."

He touched his forehead with his first finger.

"What you tell me," said the doctor, "is interesting and correct, no doubt, yet it is necessary to say definitely what kind of discomfort you experience, how it takes you . . ."

"Discomfort . . . ?"

Claude reflected a moment:

"Discomfort? . . . the word is too weak to characterize some of my feelings, too strong to define others. Sometimes I have intolerable pains in my head; sometimes, without exactly feeling any physical pain anywhere, I have strange sensations. I am obsessed by feelings that I can overcome only by force of will, when I do not succumb to them . . ."

"I am neither a roué nor a degenerate; yet there are days when certain visions rise so definitely before me and I am a prey to such violent desires, that if, hitherto, I have been able to resist their attraction, it is impossible for me to say whether, an hour hence, I shall be able to do so. At other times, I feel strangely weary, as though I had just accomplished some gigantic task. I feel that my bones are broken, my muscles torn, and it is when I wake up that I feel this—when I wake up, after eight hours' sleep and rest, following no excess and troubled by no dreams.

"I also have fits of inexplicable rage; of fury that would urge me to any crime; preconceived dislikes; I am so sensitive and excitable, that a word, a gesture, are sufficient to unhinge me: I suffer almost physically from all these things."

"What about your spirits?"

"That's terribly easy to answer: *I am unhappy*. And when I say *I am unhappy*, it is . . . although I cannot remember why . . . as definite as when other patients tell you they have a headache or cramp in the stomach.

"I have told you, Monsieur, all that I feel, all that you must believe and understand, in order for you to undertake my cure."

After these words, that had come in a rush, emphasized by trenchant gestures, and in an expressionless voice, that trembled with emotion and ill-concealed annoyance, he threw himself back in his chair, exhausted. Deep in his eyes there were evil lights, his face grew dark, and his cheeks hollow, the cheekbones stood out, accentuating the flatness of the temples, where the scanty hair, plastered down, showed a glimpse of the humid skin beneath.

"Now, let me see," said the doctor, "do you remember being seriously ill since you were a child?"

"No, unless it was before I was three or four . . . even then I should have been told."

"Will you take your clothes off?"

Claude looked surprised.

"To make sure," went on the doctor, "let me see first of all if there is anything wrong, unknown to you, which may explain your general state of health."

"Very well," he murmured.

He unbuttoned his gloves. As he drew them off, finger by finger, the doctor went on:

"Are your parents still alive?"

"Only my father . . ."

"Is it long since you lost your mother?"

"Very long."

"Do you know what she died of?"

Claude frowned and set his mouth, as though he had been asked an insulting question.

"Why do you ask me that?"

"Simply because, just as children inherit the eyes, shape of the head, and general appearance of their parents, so they may equally inherit certain mental deficiencies. If, for example, your parents had been very nervous people, the reason for your state of health would be found."

"It is not that," Claude replied in a decided voice, "no, it's not that. My father is a calm, matter-of-fact man. As for my mother, no one who ever mentioned her to me, has made the least allusion to what you suppose . . ."

"Let's try something else then. You tell me you never had a serious illness, but have you ever experienced any violent emotion, have you never been through some mental crisis, disappointment in love, or with regard to your career?"

"No."

"You never remember being frightened as a child?"

"Again, no."

"You have never heard that when your mother was enceinte, she went through any such crisis, or felt any such fear?"

Claude shook his head. This interrogation, which disturbed the ghosts of his childhood and stirred his memories, troubled him.

For the first time his thoughts were being directed toward thrilling problems; the unexpected vista hurt him.

He had answered "no" to everything without being sure. Now he was beginning to think.

He went on undressing. Bending over him, the doctor stopped him:

"What's the matter with your hands?"

"My hands?"

He stared at his open fingers.

The doctor drew back the blinds, opened the shutters, and in the broad light of day, the hands appeared.

They were strange hands indeed! Long, carefully manicured and slender, their violent color standing out in sharp contrast to the white wrists.

They were red; not with the red-brown of sunburn, nor the purplish red of a delicate skin roughened by east winds, nor were they the bright scarlet as is sometimes the case when the hands are constantly in icy-cold water. They were of a uniform, shining red, with, here and there, patches of unblemished skin, specks and stains such as might be caused by splashes of blood. And as the doctor held them outspread on his own, Claude jeered:

"I suppose there's no connection between these stains and my condition?"

"No. It's mere curiosity."

"I was wondering," he muttered between his teeth, then submitted with a bad grace to the examination.

The doctor took a pin.

"Shut your eyes . . . what am I doing?"

"You're pricking me, of course!"

"And now?"

"You're pricking me . . . you're still pricking me."

"Good . . . You may dress again . . . You don't drink?"

"No."

"The only treatment I can order you for the moment is to avoid worry and fits of temper, to take cold baths, and plenty of exercise: in one word, to tire yourself out. Fatigue is the best sedative. Eat little . . . and think less."

He rose, and with his hand on Claude's shoulder, and his clear gaze bent upon the patient's shifty glance, he added:

"And you will get well . . . do you understand . . . you must get well."

"I have not told you all, doctor," said Claude with sudden decision. "What I have to ask you exceeds the limits of a consultation, but I beg you to answer me quite plainly. I am engaged; is it right for me, in my present state, to get married?"

"Why not? Marriage will give you the regular life which you need."

"Now that's the first comforting word I have heard for a long time," cried Claude.

When he reached the street again, the sun had gone down.

He began to walk with his hands in his pockets, going over and over again in his mind, the questions asked, and the answers given.

It was certain that the man had said:

"You will get well, you must get well."

Such words are not lightly spoken. A clever doctor does not risk the contradiction of his assertions by events, just to please a patient. "He would get well, he must get well!" Infinite peace descended upon him. For one moment he felt that his will would get the better of his trouble.

His heels struck the pavement, marking time with his rapid walk. Suddenly the doubt which continually obsessed him fell headlong at his feet.

"On what evidence did that doctor give me any reassurance? . . . On what I myself told him? . . . Supposing I had not told him the truth, what then? . . . He asked me about my mother . . . I remember nothing about her . . . About my father . . . What do I know about him? . . . I spent my childhood at school, and the holidays in the country with servants. Since I have been grown-up, I never see my father except at meals. We have lived together without knowing or caring for one another; occasionally I have had a glimpse of his thoughts, but I have never linked up with them . . . What then?"

He began to tremble. Then he rebelled again:

"My mother, maybe . . . but my father? . . . Does he not look a strong, healthy man?"

At once the vision of the fair idiot child whom he had seen in the doctor's waiting-room took possession of him. Her parents looked quite strong and healthy, too. What was the dark blemish that slumbered in the impenetrable shadow of the past, and sparing the parent, destroyed the child?

He stopped with bent head, then started off again, and people turned around to look at him, surprised at his gestures and the scattered words that fell from his lips. He walked like this for a long time, crossed boulevards, the Rue Richelieu, the Cour du Carrousel and along the Seine. Twilight had come. Under the arches lights shone, their reflection dancing on the water.

He went on, turning over a thousand thoughts, trying to find, in the little he knew of his people, the gleam of light that would guide him to the source of his trouble. He passed beyond Notre-Dame. The sour smell of the Halle aux Vins irritated him. Near the gates of the Jardin des Plantes, he slackened speed, sniffing in the wild-beast smell, without noticing that there were fewer passers-by, that there was less noise, that every one had disappeared, and that nothing was left on the deserted bank of the river except the heaps of sand piled up beside the police-boats. Overpowering fatigue laid hold of him. He sat down at the water's brink, dangling his legs, and watched the river flow past.

Cries, and the sound of running footsteps aroused him from his torpor. A band of children was coming down the bank, in pursuit of a dog. The creature looked at him with an expression that was almost human in its agony; already the children had almost overtaken it.

Claude guessed what they were going to do, and that the torture of the poor dog was to end there. At any other time, he would have picked up the animal, and driven off the children. Today the thought did not even enter his head. One of them seized the dog, and held it poised. The poor beast had not even strength to bark, and fell, open-mouthed into the river. The cold water renewed its strength momentarily, and it tried to swim, and save its life.

All that Claude needed to do to save its life was to stretch out a hand. Close to him, the children jeered:

"He's sinking! He's sinking!"

The dog's muzzle disappeared first, then appeared again. A cry rang through the darkness, a ripple spread to the bank, the water curled into little waves that lost themselves in the calm of mid-river. One of the children shouted:

"He's done for!"

Then, as though roused from a nightmare, Claude stood up, raising his hands to strike:

"Little devils!"

The children took to their heels.

Looking first at the smooth surface of the water, and then at the shadows that flew along the road before him, ashamed of having allowed such a thing to be, and even to have, in some manner, enjoyed it, he went away, muttering:

"They are only children . . . But I, I am a man!"

On reaching the station of Austerlitz, he took out his handkerchief and wiped his forehead. As he raised it to his face, he saw his red hands in the light of a street lamp. Then, seized with sudden terror, he hid them under his armpits, and fled.

II

"WHAT time is it?"
"Eleven o'clock, Monsieur."
"You should not have let me sleep so late."

"Monsieur went to bed so late last night, and when I came in this morning, you were sleeping so well, I did not like to wake you."

"Open the shutters. What kind of day is it? . . ."

"Beautiful."

When the curtains were drawn back, light filled the room. A puff of balmy air came in through the open window. The leaves of the trees stood out against the calm, blue sky, and the golden daylight, the twittering of birds and the noises in the street below, filled the room with the joy of summer-time.

Claude exclaimed:

"Ah! How good it all is. Quick, my bath . . . I'll go out before lunch . . . Any news in the papers? Nothing? That's good . . . any letters?"

"One."

"Give it here . . ."

Leaning on his elbow, he tore open the envelope, read one page, and suddenly throwing off the coverings, jumped out of bed.

"Is my father in?"

"He was going down as I came up," replied the man.

"Ask him to be good enough to wait until I come down."

He threw on a few clothes and went downstairs, and into the dining-room. M. de Marbois was wiping his mouth as he pushed away his empty cup. Lighting a cigar, he said mockingly:

"Is the house on fire?"

Claude held out the letter, saying in a stifled voice: "Read that!"

M. de Marbois glanced through it rapidly as he would a document that did not interest him in the least:

> Dear Sir,
>
> After serious thought, I have decided not to allow the proposed marriage between you and my daughter to take place. I beg you not to take this decision, which in no way affects the very true regard I have for you personally, as an insult. My opinion is that you are both too young, to bind yourselves, and my concern for your welfare is the sole reason that guides me.
> Believe me . . .

Having finished reading, M. de Marbois returned the letter to his son.

"What do you say about it?" asked Claude.

"Good gracious! what I say is that M. Lesquenne does not seem to me destitute of a certain amount of common-sense, and that nothing in his letter justifies such a state of commotion on your part."

"The fact that my life is broken . . . my hopes destroyed, is nothing then?"

"Your life is not broken, neither are your hopes destroyed, because this marriage is cancelled. Do you really love this girl?"

"Love her! . . . love her, did you say?"

For the space of a second, Claude was puzzled. When he came to think about it, was it really love, or only one of his many moods, that succeeded one another, affecting his mind for a short time, and then disappearing without any trace of their presence? . . . His father's tone, and still more the attitude he had adopted goaded him to protest:

"Yes, I love her, you know I do, and so does her father. Anyone who has seen us together must know it."

M. de Marbois flicked off the ash at the end of his cigar:

"Maybe she doesn't love you?"

Claude shrugged his shoulders.

"You're joking! No, it's something else. An engagement is not broken off like this, without giving any reason. This letter is made up of hollow phrases, and vague words . . . Money and position are unquestionable on both sides; all that was settled before the formal proposal was made . . . So what is it? . . . You must go and see him . . ."

"Hum!" murmured M. de Marbois.

"Is not that your opinion?"

"I'm thinking . . . it is a very delicate matter . . ."

"A delicate matter for a father to demand an explanation?"

"No . . . it's no good . . . I can't do it . . ." broke in M. de Marbois rising. "Besides I was very never keen on the marriage, and am not sorry to see it fall through."

"And so you advise me to accept this refusal?"

"Yes."

"And not to seek the reason for it?"

"Yes."

"So you are satisfied with it! It is my opinion that you are both too young! You do not see the insult? But if you had been told the worst possible things about a man, you would express yourself in exactly the same way! Someone has been running me down to M. Lesquenne, and to Suzanne; what have they said? I do not know, but I will know, I promise you . . . unless . . . I fall back into the shadow, in which I have been struggling so many years . . ."

M. de Marbois shrugged his shoulders:

"Got it again!"

"I've never been without it," cried Claude. "For years, since I was old enough to think, nothing has been clear around me. I remain in darkness and ignorance about the most trivial details of my life. I go through life like a blind man. I take a step forward . . . and suddenly I am up against it. I go back, the shadow draws back with me. I go forward again, it precedes me! This sort of thing may go on for minutes or for weeks. At last, when I have dared everything to catch sight of the obstacle, when I have done my utmost to overcome it, I find that it is unsurmountable. I clench my fists, I stamp, I weep, and when, at last my strength fails me, my will gives way, I go round it . . . and I pass on! Only I pass on with the Unknown against which I struggle before me, and behind me the Unfathomed, whose shadow spreads out at each step I take, and leaps over my head!"

"What nonsense!"

"It's easy to say that. When I was a child, did I ever

know one of the pleasures of children of my own age? I was four when my mother died, and I can remember just enough of her to know that I used to see her weep. How many times since I've asked the cause of those tears! . . . the answer was always the same: 'she is inclined to melancholy' . . . And there are so many others things that I cannot remember! Now at last I am a man; I meet a girl whom I love and who loves me; I believe that I have found the road to happiness. I ask her to marry me. One fine morning, goodbye to all my dreams, to all the plans and promises: all is over. And thus from childhood to manhood. If I had anything to reproach myself with . . . but there is nothing. Anyone can inquire into my life without finding the least thing to complain of. Have you ever had to complain of me? Have I ever caused you annoyance, or worry? . . . Then, why, why . . . ?"

Suddenly, his voice changed, and became timid, almost pleading:

"Forgive me for what I am going to say. This thing that has just happened is so unexpected, so painful, that you cannot be angry with me for imagining the most ridiculous things . . ."

"What things?"

"I hardly like to say . . . I am sure they are absurd . . . But suppose . . . it's only a supposition . . . that there were something in your life . . . oh, nothing serious, just one of those ridiculous stories that cling to a man . . . I really do not know quite how to put it . . . Suppose . . . Help me . . . Understand what I leave unsaid . . . It is so painful to put into words . . . Do you follow me?"

"With the greatest interest," murmured M. de Marbois, with his chin in his hand.

Claude continued:

"If that were it, of course everything would be explained. I do not know how to say pretty things . . . I am not reproaching you, but you never encouraged me to show my feelings and I am as capable of filial affection as another . . . as open to decent feelings . . . And listen, I am going to say an extraordinary thing. If I were certain that M. Lesquenne were, indirectly, aiming at you, I feel sure that, far from being angry, I should care for you all the more, because of your sorrow, because of my duty to make your life happier . . . I should forget that you have not always been very kind to me . . . It is quite conceivable that a man who has suffered should retire within himself . . . In short, I should never have a bitter word or a sigh of regret, and I would blot out of my mind all that you had told me, as I respectfully beg you to banish from your mind the question I hardly dare ask."

"Look here! what are you talking about? . . . You forgive me?"

"Please don't be angry!"

"That's enough!" cried M. de Marbois. "I forbid you to speak to me in that tone. I really don't know what keeps me from pitching you outside for daring to suggest such things. I advise you not to do it again, or . . ."

"And that is all your answer?" said Claude. "Very well, I was wrong. Then there is no excuse for you, and I need not pick my words. If a father has certain rights, he also has certain duties, and at this moment you are forgetting them . . ."

Without allowing him time to finish his sentence, M. de Marbois seized him by the collar:

"Let's settle this once and for all! For twenty years I have put up with your crafty temper, and your shifty look. For twenty years I have endured you. And to reward my twenty years' patience you dare to raise your voice? . . . What do you think you are? . . . What good are you? . . . What satisfaction have I ever had out of you? . . . The moment you grew up, ought you not to have taken yourself off? You are not even fit to earn your own living! . . . you good-for-nothing, you waster, you cannot even make use of your hands! Look at them! . . . look at your hands! . . . are you not ashamed of yourself? The hands of a man of twenty-seven who must be fed and clothed! Look at them! . . ."

Claude looked attentively at his father, and at his hands, and said:

"I am looking at them!"

Then freeing himself with a violent effort, he raised his clenched fist:

"Let me go, will you!"

A mad rage had taken possession of him. He felt that his hand was going to strike, that he was an instrument of murder, and the feeling expressed itself in his face. Something terrible must have flashed from his eyes, for his father started back. But it was gone like lightning. Master of himself once more, M. de Marbois took a cigarette, lighted it slowly, took a step toward the door, looked his son up and down, and said with a sneer:

"Madman!"

Claude turned his head, and saw himself in the mirror. He was still standing in a threatening attitude. His face was livid, his eyelids bistred, his trembling lips were as white as his face, and he was afraid of his own reflection.

In his rage, he had dug the nails of his hands into his palms; with scared eyes he watched the drops of blood trickling down. Then, gradually, calm returned to him. Feeling nothing now but utter weariness, he sat down, and went over the scene that had just taken place, repeating the words his father had said, and his own replies, as though he wished to stamp them on his memory. He reviewed it all with a coolness of which he hardly believed himself capable. His fury had abated. He clearly examined cause and effect, and was astonished to find that he did not blame himself. Only an hour before, the idea of a son defying his father would have horrified him; now his attitude appeared excusable.

Did he regret it? No, indeed. He had defied his father, had insulted him, he had lifted his hand against him, with the feeling that the slightest thing would make him strike the blow. And the impulse caused him neither shame nor remorse. Deep down in his heart, he would have preferred to condemn the act. But no! All he could confess to was a regret at having given in to one of those impulses, against which he was always struggling, and which until today, he had been able to conquer.

Why, when it was his father who was in question, had his will failed him for the first time? And he repeated aloud:

"I have lifted my hand against my father! I have lifted my hand against my father!"

The words left him cold.

The footman came in:

"Will Monsieur take lunch?"

At first he did not reply, his thoughts becoming absolutely engrossed by other things.

"What claim have you on me? Since you are grown up, ought you not to be earning your own living? What good are you here? . . . I endure you . . ."

He looked at the dining-room, the windows, the furniture. How far removed it all was! And yet he had lived here for many long years, memories slumbered in every corner . . .

Through the bay window, looking down on the garden, came the stifling heat that precedes a thunderstorm. What had become of the exquisite morning freshness?

In the heavy atmosphere he felt terribly alone; he felt that everything was strange to him, that he was a stranger to all things, and an indescribable discomfort took hold of him. He remembered a day like this, when, as a tiny child, he had stood in this same dining-room and watched his mother's coffin pass out. He fancied he could see the poor dead woman; his present grief melted into the great sorrow of the past and, filled with intense self-pity, he murmured:

"Mother! Oh, mother!"

The footman said to him a second time:

"Will Monsieur take lunch?"

He answered:

"No."

As he passed the mirror he saw his face again. It was quite calm now, his eyes were heavy with fatigue, and two tears ran down his cheeks.

III

CLAUDE went up to his room, drew the curtains, and threw himself on his bed.

The subdued light that surrounded him seemed still too bright. Even under his half-closed eyes he felt the caress of the daylight shining out brightly, or growing dimmer as a cloud hurried across the sun. He was full of perplexity, his ideas were so confused that he could not follow them as they joined together, broke away, and grouped themselves anew, the wise mingling with the ridiculous, the real with the impossible. He got up—closed the shutters, and waited.

By degrees, his whirling thoughts slackened speed, and he deliberately began to examine his position.

After believing he was cured, he had awakened worse than the day before. He had dreamed of a new life, of looking after himself, conquering his incomprehensible fits of temper, and his incomprehensible fits of weakness. Nothing now remained of the plans he had made. The breaking off of his marriage destroyed all hope of settling down. He had to face this sorrow as he had had to face all others . . . alone. Instead of the help he had expected from his father, he had met with icy indifference. And yet, what dreams he had woven around that love of his! How many times he had seen that house, where, when evening came, his wife would be waiting for him. How he had longed for that facile happiness, possessed by so many who could not appreciate sweetness as he would!

It could not be. No one had the right to destroy the happiness of two beings, thus, with the stroke of a pen. He sat up and, in the friendly darkness, elaborated a plan. He would go to M. Lesquenne, would see him, speak to him, so that he would have to come back on his decision. He would tell him all his troubles, his father's selfishness, his unhappy childhood . . . He stopped, thought again, and made up his mind:

"I will go! . . . I'm going at once . . ."

Immediately a thousand objections rose before him.

"Suppose he will not see me? Suppose he has gone away? Suppose he does see me, and when I have said all I have to say, tells me that his decision is irrevocable?"

He went over the imaginary scene in his mind, arranging the smallest details of it, and murmured:

"Yes, that is exactly what will happen!"

His thoughts then followed in logical order, and he asked himself what her attitude would be . . . Strange to say, from that moment, his defeat seemed to him inevitable. He gaged the instability of their love. How is it possible to know a girl from what one sees of her in society? When it came to himself, had he sufficient experience of life to know what words to choose in dealing with a stranger who has to learn everything from you? He no longer attempted to think of what means they had employed to induce her to go back on her promise, what revelation had sufficed to make her give up her promised bliss. He had no strength left in him to seek and, if he had, what would be the use of it . . . ?

Fate, chance, were against him, through no fault of his. Things were so, simply because they were so. He carried upon his thin shoulders a burden beneath which he bent more at every step he took. Perhaps there was an unlucky sign on his forehead, visible to all save himself! Because he had never struggled against the hard blows of Fate, he felt himself hopelessly beaten now. It was not defeat after battle, not a complete rout during which the vanquished gallop madly away under torrents of shell, men and horses falling by the way. Defeat of that kind lends a tragic grandeur even to the din that accompanies it. His own defeat was more sinister, it was endless despondency, like that of an army each soldier of which is less fearful than ashamed, and he blushed at the thought of his misery as though it were a sin, at his solitude as though it were a crime, and at his grief as though it were a cowardly act.

The best part of the afternoon had gone. Pale twilight followed on the heat of late afternoon. The end of the day brings with it a langourousness that affects both people and things. Just as the poorest village puts on a youthful aspect with the morning light, so, in spite of the noise and movement, and the last golden rays of the sun, an unsuspected feeling of despair creeps into the heart when twilight falls. Lovers prefer it to the night, because it brings an added languor to their gestures, an added sweetness to their dreams; weak souls love it for its weariness and calm. Broad day and deep night are made for active passion, but it is at eventide that one may know the depths of despair.

For a moment Claude remained still. His eyes wandered over the familiar furniture, over the pictures that hung on the walls. This room contained nothing that was dear to him, nothing that so much as recalled a pleasure;

the shadow that deepened between these four walls was no less profound than the shadow which never left him. Then what good was it to go on living, to wait for tomorrows that were always the same as today, brushing against the skirts of happiness but never grasping it? Why take care of himself? Why get better? Live? For whom?

He thought to himself:

"Yes, that is the best . . . indeed the only thing!"

He rose, opened a drawer of his bureau, and took out a revolver. Drawing it from its case, he examined the barrel, manipulated the magazine, and said:

"There!"

He repeated in different tones:

"There! There!"

Satisfied that his voice did not tremble, his hand did not shake, he smiled as he put in the cartridges.

The weapon was before him. It did not look very terrible—a pretty little toy with its black handle and shining barrel. Presently he would raise it to his temples; one movement, and all would be over.

He took the revolver in his hand, lifted it to the level of his eyes, and stared into the little open mouth of the barrel. Without moving his hand he turned his head to bring his temple near it. It was easy, very easy indeed, as easy as an irrevocable word or gesture.

The clock on the mantelpiece was ticking out his last seconds: it was ten minutes to seven. Looking again at the revolver which he still held in his hand, he thought:

"Ah, yes! it is easy, and quickly over . . . In a moment! . . ."

He replaced it on the mantle, and without asking himself: "why not at once?" decided to wait until the clock struck the hour. In setting a limit to his life, thus, he felt himself the greater for the power that was his to do away with himself at the chosen moment.

He who had never been master of the smallest thing: he who had never been able to say, "I will," had never known a desire to succumb to his command, he whom life had ever humbled, and tossed hither and thither, was about to demonstrate his liberty, his will, his strength, for the first time in his life, by putting an end to everything, destroying everything, departing this life . . .

How marvelous!

Going away, setting forth . . .

He sought words to express himself without having to say the word "to die," which seemed too violent, and too decisive . . .

It was five minutes to seven by the clock. The moment approached. He looked round him as one does when starting on a journey, to make sure that nothing is left behind.

And suddenly he burst into a fit of laughter. Yes, he was forgetting what he had longed for so desperately just now in the dining-room, he was also forgetting the burden of remorse and hatred that he wished to leave behind him. Go away like that, quietly? That, surely, would be too absurd! so that his father might feign grief, and say:

"The poor boy shot himself in a moment of nervous stress. He who had everything to make him happy . . ."

No! a hundred times no! He would first write down the tortures of his childhood, the sorrows of his manhood, so that people would know why he had preferred death to a life without love or pity. The thought that the blame would fall on his father, that the scandal would cause that hard, proud being to tremble, filled him with joy:

The clock struck, and fear, mingled with a touch of regret and pity, entered into his soul. But what were fear and pity against admirable vengeance? He did not fear the words "to die" any longer, feeling that their horror weighed less on him than on his father. When all was said and done, what did he care about life and death? The one a weariness; the other annihilation . . . Pah!

Alone, he might have found in his indifference or his weakness the courage one needs to go on living. But from the moment he had offered himself the joy of leaving such a heritage behind him, he was no longer alone.

He began to write. The words, which a moment ago had come into his mind with ease, now refused themselves. He could not remember the phrases he made up; those he wrote down did not express his thoughts or, at best, expressed them badly. Ten times did he begin a letter, ten times did he tear it up, and, at last, fearing lest he should be disturbed, he wrote on a clean sheet of paper:

"I leave to him who has made it inevitable, the responsibility of my suicide."

Night had come. The twittering of the birds in the garden came more intermittently. Remembering that those who have been on the brink of death say that in one instant the whole of their life passed before their eyes, he wished to see his memories again. But the shadow was within as well as around him, and vainly he bent his gaze on the darkness of his past.

Then fear at the thought of the dread journey took him; the darkness was peopled with forms and the silence with sounds. Without tightening his grasp on the revolver, he felt the grooves in the handle against the palm of his hand, so plainly that he counted them, and he stared at his motionless hand with terror, thinking:

"Will it place itself of its own accord against my forehead, in spite of me, before I am ready? . . ."

A force was urging him to the brink, and he pleaded: "Not yet." The whole of life . . . not his life, was dancing around him. Voices struck his ears, soothed him and led him back, while others murmured: "Go!" . . . He felt himself grow weaker, wished to be strong, and to whip up his courage said aloud:

"I will not live any longer!"

The cold circle of the barrel pressed against his temple. He felt the roundness of it. Never had his brain been clearer. The clock was ticking rapidly. In the street below a newsboy was calling out the evening papers. The barrel pressed harder, as though a hand had guided his. The steel grew warm as it remained in contact with the flesh. He did not feel it any longer, and counted . . .

"One . . . two . . ."

Suddenly, he saw a vision of his body lying prone across the table, of a little trickle of blood on the mahogany, of his limp arms, his nerveless hands, his staring eyes . . . Now he was only a thing, worthless . . . He stood upright, crying: "No! no! . . . not that! . . ." flung down the revolver, and breathed with the relief and delight of a man who has just escaped mortal danger.

When the lamp was lighted, his room, with the unmade bed, closed shutters, and garments lying across a chair, did not seem so dismal. He saw the strip of paper on which he had written a few minutes since, and put it in his pocket: that was over, nothing remained to show what he had tried to do; he was alive. He was going to live!

At once the image of Death stood before him, tranquil and almost gentle. But already he looked upon it from afar. It retreated before him with each beat of his heart, and as it disappeared, he was filled with a great depression, a shame at his cowardice, and a disgust at his weakness. He thought of Death with a two-fold fear of seeing it disappear, and of feeling, once again, its arms around his neck. Then all vanished, and, alone at last, he sighed:

"Life continues around me, and I shall have to submit to it, seeing that I have not had the courage to kill myself."

Someone knocked at his door; he started:

"What is it?"

"Monsieur wishes to know if you are dining, Sir?"

"Well! Well!" he thought, "he's beginning to reckon with me now, is he?"

This was the first time his father had inquired for him. Generally, when Claude went into the dining-room, his father did not even turn his head, and when he rose to go to his club, remarked,

"You were there, were you? Goodnight."

Claude was surprised at this new departure, and was on the point of replying:

"No, I am dining out."

But he thought better of it, dressed, and went down to the dining-room.

With a strange revulsion of thought he half repented, and almost regretted his violence that morning. Who could tell? Perhaps his father was merely one who acted on impulse, like himself, and to whom it was only fair to forgive a hasty word. Perhaps he had gone back on his decision. Suppose, after having refused to do so, he had decided to seek the interview! . . .

The last thought gave him no pleasure.

When he had heard his marriage was broken off, he felt it to be a disaster; but now that seemed an old story, forgotten . . . In any case, he had accepted it.

An hour since, what he had called "his dream" had gone out of his life, even more easily than it had entered it, and the mere thought of beginning it all over again, instead of pleasing, worried him. It had been sufficient for him to contemplate the prospect of his lonely life, for the idea of a companion, even the woman he had believed he loved, to break down the balance of the calm into which his soul had plunged anew. Therefore, if his father were to say: "It's all arranged!" what attitude should he adopt? His answer was soon ready. Without allowing him to complete his sentence, to express a regret, he would stop him:

"Thank you, but now I think as you do. I am happy as I am, I will not marry . . ."

And as he went downstairs, he told himself that the morning's scene had done some good after all, as it had brought his father nearer to him. It made him think a little of the prodigal son; the question asked by the footman marked the first step towards reconciliation, towards a changed life, and with his hand on the door, he smiled:

"I wonder if my father will ever know that he very nearly never saw me again? . . ."

And he rejoiced that the fear of annihilation had stayed his hand, and went in timidly, almost happy.

But he stopped short, as though frozen to the spot. His father had finished dinner and was reading the paper. On the table, which had been half cleared, his napkin was thrown down beside an empty cup, containing the blackened end of a cigarette. His own place was laid on the other side, and his chair drawn up; the same scene as every evening, the dinner like every other dinner, quickly served, and silent. Then why had he sent for him?

The footman was offering him a dish; he refused:

"No soup."

His father put down the paper and remarked in an indifferent tone;

"I have something to say to you."

Claude signed to the servant to stop waiting on him.

"We can talk quite well while you are eating," said M. de Marbois.

He lighted his cigar, and went on:

"I do not know whether you have thought over our conversation. I have done so, and it seems necessary for us to come to some understanding on the subject . . ."

Claude bowed in assent.

"For one in your condition, the best thing for your health and well-being, is to live secluded—a rational secluded life, under supervision, under . . . how shall I put it . . . under the eye of a medical man, in some quiet spot, far from the noise of a city, where influenced by someone with a strong will, surrounded by the care you need, you will find, for the first time in your life, the balance of your faculties, the right notion of your duties, in one word, a cure . . . Do you understand me?"

Claude bit his lip. He was playing with his knife, mechanically, and his hand began to shake so much that the blade rattled against the edge of the plate. His father repeated:

"Do you understand me?"

He shook his head and said:

"No."

"It is rather difficult to explain . . . you are not in a fit state to grasp certain niceties, or to appreciate certain necessities. The doctor I saw a short while since, and whom you will see tomorrow, will explain."

Claude grew white, and looked over his shoulder. The servant waited, motionless, behind him. He opened his mouth to tell him to go out of the room, but thought better of it. He understood the cold cruelty of which his father had broached such a conversation before a third person; he particularly understood the calculation that had made him speak before a witness, who could intervene, if need be, or relate any loss of temper on his part, and he grew calm again.

The game was too simple, and the malice too obvious! On his side, he had the strength of a man who waits, who watches, who can force the enemy to lay bare his thoughts, and he said frankly:

"No, really, I cannot see . . . A doctor . . . why? I am not ill . . ."

"You are."

"Do you imagine that the slight disappointment which we have already discussed has upset me to such a degree? Do fears for my health trouble you so much that you foresee . . . while exaggerating it . . . the grief it may cause me? Nothing prevents me from going away for a few weeks . . ."

M. de Marbois objected roughly:

"No, not traveling about . . . traveling means adventure, no control, and it is necessary that you be under control, that you be taken quietly, without any fuss, to a quiet spot . . . I repeat what I said before to . . ."

"To a private asylum, for instance?"

M. de Marbois tried to meet his son's eyes. They were so calm, so clear, that his own fell, and he said to the servant:

"You can come again presently. Monsieur will ring . . ."

Claude smiled. All the concentrated hatred within him appeared in that smile:

"Why? I have nearly finished. Pierre can stay . . . But if you prefer it . . . Go, Pierre, I will ring for you."

When the door closed again, he sat back in his chair, and laid his clenched hands heavily on the table:

"That fellow is neither deaf nor a fool. He heard and understood that you are trying to force me into a nursing home, in other words, into a madhouse! . . . Oh don't let the word upset you, when the intention leaves you calm. Well, however much you may wish it, I am not mad, and have no desire to become so . . ."

M. de Marbois struck the floor with his foot:

"Who ever mentioned that? . . . Is this morning's scene to begin again?"

"Oh no! Oh no! See how low and quietly I speak. I fear scandal, and dislike dumb witnesses. However great a scoundrel the doctor who gave you advice without seeing me may be, he needs rather more than your desire, supported by a few francs, to send me to the cell and the shower-bath! He needs just a tiny, tiny little certificate . . . And I wish to be free . . . do you hear, free. *It is necessary* for me to be free."

"For all the use you've made of your freedom so far!" sneered M. de Marbois.

"Maybe! but I am keen on it . . . so much so that I too have consulted a doctor, and I am going to follow a treatment, but as he wishes, and as I agree to. If I am mad, you must admit, that I am a terribly reasonable and annoying madman at this moment."

He went on, laughing:

"Why am I in your way? I can't think of a reason. For years, I have been trying to find out why, without ever having harmed a soul, never having had a vengeance to satisfy, nor a secret to hide, tortured by others and by myself, blind rages that make me shudder surge into my heart. In the same way I try to find out why I lie, as though terrible results might come from innocent truths . . ." His voice had gradually grown louder, and his eyes, so clear a moment ago, became cloudy . . .

"I feel . . . I know that within me there sleeps a terrible being, who wakes up, now and then, and fills me with dread. But it is you who made me, and it is no more my fault that I have the fair hair and pale face of the degenerate, and hands like these that look as though I had dipped them in an orgy of blood . . ."

He spread his red hands upon the tablecloth.

In his look and gesture was something so terrible that he realized it, and, recovering himself, went on with the conversation:

"But, in spite of all that, because of all that, if you prefer it, I will not go into a nursing home."

"You don't imagine, I hope, that after this morning, we can go on living together. If you object to the nursing home, we will not mention it again, but it is no less necessary for us to part company. I wish it, I insist upon it . . ."

"And so do I. I will go away."

"May I be permitted to know where?"

"To Vendée."

M. de Marbois raised his head.

"Vendée? Where? Why?"

"Where? To Saint-Fulgent. Why? Because I will take nothing from you, and with my own money I can live in the house mother left me."

"A ridiculous idea. None of us have been in the place for twenty years. The house must have fallen to pieces."

"That does not matter; no matter what it is like, I shall be comfortable there; it is my house, and it belonged to my mother."

"You know nothing about that part of the country."

"My mother loved it."

"What do you know about it?"

"She used to speak of it. That is sufficient for me."

"Do you so much as remember your mother?"

Claude's face lit up, as though a vision of the dead woman had passed before his eyes:

"I remember nothing else."

"You shall not go to Saint-Fulgent," cried M. de Marbois.

"I shall go there."

"Is that your last word?"

"My last."

"Listen; if you go there against my wish, you can make your mind that it will be for always. I refuse you nothing necessary to your health. Go to Switzerland, Italy, where you like, but . . ."

"It's no use, I shall go to Saint-Fulgent."

"How long since you decided on this?"

"Always."

M. de Marbois burst out laughing.

"Come! here's a decision that will have the same fate as all others! Tomorrow it will be something else!"

"Tomorrow I shall be gone."

M. de Marbois struck the table with his clenched fist: "Look here . . . Good God! . . . who is master here?"

Claude put his fingers to his lips.

"Gently! I have just rung for Pierre."

The footman entered. M. de Marbois had sat down again, and was biting his nails. Claude stared at him. For a moment the dreadful expression came into his eyes again; then, without a word, without turning his head, he went out.

IV

WHEN he got off the train, Claude had to stop at Montaigu, to look for a conveyance, and, while waiting for the horses to be harnessed, went into an inn on the square.

As he sipped the drink he had ordered, he looked around him. Some peasants were playing at cards; in a corner a boy was doing his lessons. Now and again the sound of sabots, or the deep clang of a blacksmith's hammer, broke the silence. Evening spread an impressive calm over the village. The man came in and said:

"The carriage is ready; we can start."

Claude stretched himself, for he was tired and stiff from the journey, sat down on the seat beside the driver, and the little horse started off.

As they passed the last houses of the village, the driver entered into conversation:

"So, Monsieur is going to Trois-Tourelles?"

"Yes. It isn't far, is it?"

"About an hour and a half."

"As much as that?"

"At least. Monsieur does not know the country, it is probably the first time he has been here?"

"Yes, my parents used to come here."

"Oh, they would remember it, for it has hardly changed. The country is not like the town. When once the houses are built, nobody touches them again. Everything remains in its place, people as well as things. The same farmers are here who were here more than forty years ago."

"I know."

"Of course if Monsieur is a friend of M. de Marbois, he knows all there is know. But M. de Marbois never comes here now. It is Chagne the tenant farmer, who is practically boss there. Sometimes, he even says he wishes the master would come along and take a look around."

"Well, he will have his wish then, for here I am!"

The man held back his horse:

"Ah . . . it is Monsieur . . . it is Monsieur's son. Look at that now! people said you were ill . . . you know how people will talk when they don't know . . . don't you?"

These words roused Claude from his indifference, and he asked:

"Who says that?"

"I've heard it said . . . and if it is rest that Monsieur is needing, he will get that at the farm, it's not so noisy there as Paris. The country is the best thing for anyone whose nerves are not strong."

Claude was not listening. Thus, wherever he went, his reputation preceded him. Even in this remote corner of the Bocage, people knew he was different from others, and this peasant who spoke of anyone *whose nerves are not strong* probably thought more than what he said. He was on the point of telling him to go back, and to catch the next train home, but he felt too tired to spend another night traveling yet. Besides, the magic of the countryside, the scent of the fields, from which came the smell of newly-turned earth, the sight of the low hedges, and sturdy oaks, everything . . . even the fresh air, the bark of a watch-dog, soothed and lulled him, like an old, old song, the words of which are forgotten, but to which we listen fondly and recognize, remembering the refrain instinctively, before it is sung, because, when we were tiny children, hardly able to speak, a sleepy nurse sang it to us, as with careless hand she rocked our cradle.

This unknown country was more familiar to him than Paris. The straight road that stretched before him brought no memories with each turning; but every time it disclosed new details, a house on the edge of a field, a pond where the oxen had trampled the mud, he said to himself:

"I feel that I have *seen these things before!*"

The carriage lamps threw little dancing lights and shadows on the road. The bells tinkled more slowly, the horse slackened speed.

"A hill," said the peasant.

At the end of the slope, a village appeared, they went down the other side, the horse picked his way, rolling from side to side, and the brake creaked along the wheels. Then they went up again. At last, crossing the village street, they turned a corner, and were amid fields, where a big farm with a huge farmyard, and uneven roofs, spread out before them.

At a distance, it looked asleep. No smoke floated from the chimneys, no light shone in any window. But as they drew nearer, they saw a tiny point of light piercing the darkness; a dog barked, awakened hens flapped their wings. A warm smell of straw litters came to them on the breeze. The light moved, disappeared, and appeared again under the door, and a voice said:

"That's enough, Tambour."

The dog stopped barking, and growled instead, and the voice inquired:

"Who is it? Where are you going?"

"Is it you, Chagne?" said the driver, "someone to see you."

"Wait!" said the man suspiciously.

"Whoa!" said the peasant, and brought his horse to a standstill. Then, turning to Claude: "I don't care about going any nearer, he's a cross-grained fellow, and would have a shot at us as soon as look! . . ."

And, as a matter of fact, Père Chagne did arrive, escourted by his dog, and carrying a gun.

He stared at the carriage, the peasant, and the traveler; Claude got down:

"Père Chagne, I am M. Claude."

"Excuse me, master," stammered the farmer, "I did not know . . ."

"Did you not receive my telegram?"

"I did receive a telegram, but I cannot read. My son is at Nantes, so I was waiting till tomorrow."

"There will always be some eggs and a glass of milk for my dinner, and a bed for me to sleep in, of course?"

"Ah, master! not eggs, we haven't got so much as one. We took them all to market, and the milk. And we don't milk again till the morning. And there isn't a bed really fit . . ."

What the man was saying was simple and comprehensible enough. Expecting no one, they had not prepared anything. Yet Claude felt furiously angry. Ever since he started, he had been thinking of his arrival at the farm. Old Chagne and all his sons assembled to welcome him, the house ready, the table set.

Instead of that they greeted him, gun in hand, nothing was prepared, everything was depressing, everything was ugly. The wrinkled old farmer impressed him disagreeably; everything here seemed hostile to him, even the dog, who sniffed around his legs growling. He struck him with his stick and sent him off, remarking in a surly voice to the peasant who had driven him: "Show me the light," and preceded by the farmer, went into the house.

The pleasant, restful feeling he had experienced during the drive was now lost in one of utter weariness, and bored surprise—in a need to hear nothing, see nothing, think of nothing, and to sleep. An old woman came out of an adjoining room:

"Wife," said the farmer, "this is our master."

The old woman became busy at once, hurried to the dresser, spread a cloth, and laid the table. She too made excuses; if they had only known, if they had only the least idea . . . but they would fix things up for tonight, and tomorrow . . .

The eagerness they showed in serving him, the regrets they reiterated, and, above all, the word "master" which recurred at nearly every other word, put him into a little better humor. Fits of anger, as well as fits of gaiety did not last long with him. He asked about the crops, the price of the cattle, in the tone of a man who wants to know how things are, as quickly as possible. The old man had gone out, the farmer stood facing him, cap in hand. From the yard came a great sound of flapping wings, and the terrified squawks of fowls. Claude got up.

In the fowlhouse, deep in shadow, where the farmer's wife was trying to catch a chicken, terror swept through the feathered world; the hens ran along, their necks outstretched, their wings wide-spread. One ran into Claude's legs; he seized it.

"No, master, not that one," said the woman, "it's an old one . . . we want a young bird. . . Look, that one. Eh! But you're more clever than I am."

The creature was squawking dismally. It would seem as though the inhabitants of the poultry-yard have a vision of their approaching end, the moment they are caught, so despairing is their outcry.

"You'll soil your hands, master," said the farmer's wife. "Give him to me, it will only take a minute."

She shut the door, and sat down on a stump of wood, put the chicken between her knees, opened his beak with one hand, and with the other, plunged in the scissors, and gave a smart cut. There was a rattle, a spurt of blood; she lifted up the chicken by its wings, holding it at arm's length, so as not to be bespattered, she let it bleed. First the blood flowed in a thin stream, then drop by drop, then more slowly, a heavier drop coagulated at the end of the beak, and all was over. While she rapidly plucked the chicken, Claude said:

"It doesn't take long."

"Well, no, master, you see it's a young one, the feathers are only down, and come out easily."

"I mean to kill it."

She explained:

"Yes, that one! but sometimes, it all depends . . . Some of them struggle. It isn't very nice to look at . . . Now it's plucked and emptied and all that remains to do is to fry it in the pan."

Claude returned with her to the kitchen, where a fire of vine branches was blazing. As he watched the preparations, he thought of the poor, terror-stricken chicken that had run against his legs. He heard its cry, its death-rattle, and as he had done the day the dog was drowned, realized that he had taken an ugly pleasure in looking on at the scene.

The butter was frizzling on the fire. The farmer's wife turned around:

"In five minutes it will all be ready . . ."

Then looking at Claude's hands, she took a towel:

"I told you, master, that you would soil your hands; your fingers are covered with blood."

Interrupted in his thoughts, Claude took the towel mechanically, but, looking at his hands, overcome by a great fear, and a great shame, he said:

"No . . . it's not blood . . . it's the color . . ."

Once again the farm, the low-ceilinged room, and the hearth, where little bits of live coal fell amid the ashes, depressed him. He ate little, drank one glass of wine, took his candle, went into the room that had been prepared for him, and to bed. He turned and tossed for a long time, between the rough sheets, unable to sleep, his ears buzzing as they do when silence succeeds prolonged noise. At last it stopped. He thought of his mother who, perhaps, had slept in that room, of the drowning dog, and the little bleeding chicken, of a thousand and one sad, confused things, then sleep came and took him.

V

CLAUDE had come to the country, like a city man would, for a few days' rest, but with the intention of living there, and finding among these simple folk the forgetfulness, and quiet happiness that come from hard work, and freedom from care.

His mother had left him the farm, left it entirely to him, with an income of 12,000 francs, a fortune in that part of the country, where, Montaigu on the one side and Fontenay-le-Comte on the other were almost big towns.

Not far from the farm was the dwelling-house, with a kitchen garden, and a fine lawn. He could live there, perfectly content, looking after the farm, and breeding cattle.

The next day, he went round his property, crossed fields, visited stables, stopping to look at the oxen sprawling on the straw.

As he was anxious to learn all he could, he expressed surprise that these should be lying at ease, lazy, fat, and well-cared for, while the others, harnessed to carts full of straw, were working with foam-flecked nostrils, and heads bent beneath the yoke.

"We are fattening these, master," explained Père Chagne. "All they have to do is sleep and eat their fill. We only want them to get fat. In two months' time they will be sold to a butcher. They will go Paris way . . . Maybe you've eaten some of your own beasts there, without knowing it . . . That cow is in calf . . . Oh, don't be afraid, they are quite gentle . . . They know their names, and are as obedient as dogs. Indeed, I am sorry to let those two over there go . . . But what's the good?"

When he had been all over the estate, drunk a glass with the laborers, patted the babies' cheeks, and looked over the muddy pond where ducks were swimming, he asked to see his house.

As they crossed a little copse, he saw it, half-hidden by two great cypress trees. Their branches covered with dark needles, almost touched. A thick growth of ivy covered the front of the house, and encroached upon the roof, and the closed shutters, washed by many rains, and roasted by many suns. Ragged plants grew all over the garden. Pale, scentless flowers were dotted among the weeds that had killed the grass, and, without the scrunching of the gravel underfoot, they would not have known that there were paths around the lawn. Everything had grown anyhow, around the empty house in its lonely corner; the trees had become gigantic, and under their shade, which increased year by year, flowers, on which the sun never shone, were but sickly growths, with ailing petals and leaves that withered quickly.

Claude looked at the rickety bench, the empty kennel, in front of which lay a rusty chain. The farmer chose a key from his bunch, and, while he thrust it in the lock, offered what he evidently considered a necessary explanation:

"It looks dismal like this, because it hasn't been kept up . . . no one ever comes here. But it is really pretty when everything is tidy. Years ago, when the paths were graveled, the beds full of flowers, and the trees cut and pruned, it was a beautiful garden. If the master will only send for a gardener, it will soon be put in order again . . ."

As he spoke, he pushed against the door with his shoulder. The wood was damp, the lock rusty, and the door would not open. He kicked it, and it turned on its hinges. Then he drew back, saying jokingly:

"It didn't want us to go in, you know . . ."

As he crossed the threshold, and encountered the damp, sour smell of the atmosphere, Claude started back.

It smelt of mildew, of old wall-paper, and of cretonne. Without putting a hand near it, it was easy to tell that the paper was soaked and velvety to the touch, and peeled off under the fingers. His voice echoed in the dark rooms, and he hardly dared move because the sound of his footsteps was so painful to the ears.

Although the sun was blazing out in the garden, the light that came in here seemed dismal. The old-fashioned drawing-room, the dining-room, the billiard-room, all breathed desertion. The pictures on the walls were covered with a thick veil of damp, so carefully laid on that it was impossible to see what was portrayed beneath; the mirrors only sent back the ghosts of reflections; nothing was out of order. The chairs, ranged in lines along the walls, were covered with moth-eaten velvet; on a small mahogany table, the dust had collected thickly, like a cover, so equal, and evenly spread, that it was easy to see no hand had disturbed it for many years.

Claude wanted to think of these rooms as they were when they were inhabited, he wanted, by a thousand and one little things, to discover the routine of the life that had been lived there.

Certainly he could see his father in the billiard-room, or seated in front of the black bureau in the big drawing-room; but which was his mother's room? What chair had she sat in, to dream, on winter evenings when the lamps were lit? For she had lived here. How well inanimate things guard their secrets!

Even children who have lost their mother when quite tiny, know her. As soon as they are old enough to understand, someone will show them a portrait, a jewel she loved, the table where she used to keep her work. They will say to them:

"At such and such a time she used to do this, at other times, that. This was her favorite place . . ." They will repeat the words she used to say. The children end by hearing the dear dead voice, by knowing what gave her pleasure, and they love her memory almost as much as they would have loved her presence.

He had known nothing of all such things. He had nothing but his memories of his mother, and, as she had died when he was four, almost before he had learned how to kiss her, to keep her deep down in the eyes of his memory, he never remembered her other than ailing, sad, and quiet.

He thought perhaps the old farmer might remember her:

"I suppose it is here my mother used to sit?"

"It depended. When she first came, she used to run about the garden, to go to the farm, and amuse herself looking after the animals, and feeding the fowls. She was very merry . . . Afterwards . . . well . . ."

"Yes, when she fell ill, after my birth . . ."

"Well, not exactly . . ."

He hesitated, and went on in a lower voice:

"Not exactly . . . not exactly . . ."

Claude did not notice the hesitation and embarrassment of the worthy man. He was thinking:

"That's it. There was no reason for her sadness. I am like her, and, like her I shall depart, fed-up, tired of life . . . Poor mother! . . ."

Ah, how he loved her at that moment, the mother, who used to fondle him, and smooth his hair with her white hands, saying softly, tenderly: "Poor little fellow!" in exactly the same voice as he had said: "Poor mother!"

And, with a longing to get nearer to her, to feel her presence through the mystery of time and space, he inquired:

"Do you remember her, Père Chagne?"

"As though I saw her before me."

"Am I like her?"

"Oh! no . . ."

Seeing that his young master was hurt by his reply, he corrected himself:

"Perhaps you are something like her . . . after all."

"At any rate, I am not like my father?"

"Oh no! that's very certain . . . oh, no, no . . ."

This assertion filled him with the deepest joy.

VI

FOR two months Claude lived with no other care than that of watching the grass grow, the wheat ripen, and the vines sprout. When the grass and the wheat were cut, and the grapes gathered, he watched the approach of autumn.

The weather was still summer-like, but the nights, which were drawing in, heralded winter. The fields, where nothing now interrupted the view, spread out to right and left, the hill-sides covered themselves in fog, and the forest clothed itself in the red-brown tint of a newly baked loaf. By degrees Nature was teaching him her joys, and her secrets, filling him with wonder.

He saw none but the farm people, and thoroughly enjoyed sharing their quiet life. The children amused him, and sometimes he would sit for long hours besides the herds, silent like them, learning the cries that call the cattle together, or rouse the attention of absent-minded dogs. One day he stopped beside a brook whither a girl was leading some cattle.

She was sixteen or seventeen, with rough hands, and sunburned arms, round hips that undulated as she walked; her bosom swelled under her tight blouse, and her face was covered with freckles, and laughed at him from under her tangled eyes.

The day before he had hovered near her, without daring to address her with the same shyness that made him hesitate to speak to a girl in Paris. She saw him as he passed along, blushed and said:

"Good-day, master!"

He replied:

"Good-day, my child."

Politely, she picked up her bag, the pointed stick she used as a goad, and her ball of wool, stuck through with knitting-needles, and prepared to go away. He held her back:

"Are you afraid of me, child?"

"No, master."

He began to laugh, and sat down on a tree trunk; she remained standing, and he said:

"There's room beside me."

She took up her knitting again, and sat down. He asked her:

"Do you often come here?"

"Of course, master, you know very well I do."

She meant nothing by this, and did not intend him to know she had noticed his by-play, but only to express the thought, that as he was the master, who knew everything that was going on on his estate, he must also know that. He did not understand her meaning, and blushed in his turn. He had always been timid with women, and the ragged dress of this one did not prevent him from feeling confused. With an unexpected fusion of ideas, the memory of his fiancée crossed his mind, and, suddenly, without the least idea why this question came to his lips, he said:

"Are you going to be married soon, child?"

She looked at him:

"I don't know."

"Haven't you got a sweetheart?"

"I've no time for that."

The answer amused him, the girl looked prettier, and he took her hand. He was going to speak again, when a voice made her raise her head:

"Hi, Marie! Come and do the washing . . . the boy will look after the cattle."

She rolled up her stocking, took her bag and the white stick, and got up. Claude was annoyed at her departure, and murmured as he would have done to a lady in a drawing-room:

"You'll come again tomorrow?"

She did not reply and joined her father. Claude hailed the old man:

"Are you all right, Père Gravelot?"

"If it pleases you, master."

And, touching his cap, the old man pushed his daughter along in front of him.

Since then, he had often returned to the same spot, pensively, with burning head and twitching fingers, a prey to desires which he could neither express nor wholly disguise. But such shades of feeling are more within the scope of town rather than country women, and this country girl did not seem to notice them, unless it amused her to watch the growth of his fancy . . .

Time passed, the shooting season began, and, as much for the sake of forgetting a flirtation that was absorbing his time as for the pleasure of something new, Claude no longer came to the meadow beside the water.

Old Chagne had taught him how to fill cartridges; every evening, he sat at his table, beside the lighted lamp, and got his provision ready for the next day. As soon as daylight came, he was off across the plain. One day, when jumping across a ditch, he clumsily caught his gun in something, and it went off, just breaking the skin of his hand. As he had neither bandages nor antiseptic with him, he went to M. Coutelet, the village apothecary.

This was an old man with a reputation for learning. The country people asked his advice before consulting a doctor, and after doing so, consulted him forthwith, to find out if the prescription was any good. Claude knew him by sight, having caught a glimpse of him bending over his counter in the dim light of his shop, weighing out powders and ointments with careful fingers, and he had often wondered about the old man, with his long hair, and clean-shaven face.

He went in; a peasant was waiting for some medicine that was being made up.

"Your servant, Sir," said the apothecary, and stopped tapping a bottle, "what can I do for you?"

"Only to bind up my hand . . . but finish with this good man first."

He sat down and looked at the jars that stood in a line on the shelves. As he finished what he was doing. M. Coutelet gave the peasant advice:

"Give a dose every hour to your wife . . . and don't let her go out on any account."

He shook the bottle, corked it carefully, gummed on a label, crinkled a green paper cap for it with his nimble fingers, gave it to the man, and went to the door with him.

"Now, Monsieur, I am at your service."

"It's only a scratch," said Claude, untying the handkerchief in which he had swathed his hand, "a fragment of powder tore the skin a little . . ."

"A little! Plague take it! You're pretty cool about it! Why your hand is covered with blood."

"No, no, it's a scratch, I tell you. It's here . . . the rest is the color of my skin."

"Ah, that's very curious," cried M. Coutelet. "Will you allow me to look? It is really strange."

Claude frowned. He did not care to have too much notice taken of this peculiarity. The apothecary made no further remark, took a wad of cotton-wool, sponged away the blood, and while he spread a square piece of lint on the little wound, said:

"You're passing through here, I expect?"

"No, I'm living at Trois-Tourelles."

The old man looked up:

"So, you're M. de Marbois? I might have known . . ."

"Why?"

"Because you don't look like one of our village folk."

He placed one end of bandage on the hand and rolled it around.

"Have you lived long at Saint-Fulgent?" asked Claude.

"Forty-seven years," answered the old man; "it's a lease, you see. You are surprised to think anyone can exist in such a hole, when life is so full of activity in Paris. But you don't make your life, it is served out to you. I came here when I had finished my studies, to wait for something better. And the waiting has lasted nearly half a century. But when all's said and done, it does not matter where you live, provided you *do* live. When you have your books, your microscope, and your memories, when you do all the good you can . . ."

"I believe you are right," said Claude, "and I myself have made up my mind to live at Saint-Fulgent."

"You have a fine property, and plenty to keep you busy. If you take the trouble, you will make money out of your estate. The country-people round here are honest and hard-working, but behind the times. I have studied different methods of modern agriculture, and if I had the time and money . . . But perhaps if I had the one, I should not have the other," he finished with a laugh.

"You're a philosopher."

"Philosophy is the tip life leaves you, when on the point of departing, Monsieur Claude."

"You know my Christian name?"

"I carry all the parish registers in my head."

"You probably knew my parents then?"

"I knew your mother best," replied M. Coutelet, with a slight hesitation; "she was not very strong . . . poor lady . . ."

"Alas!" murmured Claude. "And did you know my father too?"

"Not so well . . ."

"What a voice!"

"We had not the same political opinions," M. Coutelet explained, "my plain speaking had something to do with that . . ."

"Don't excuse yourself; I understand all the more that people do not get along with him, because I . . ."

"In short, we were not in sympathy," concluded M. Coutelet as he dried his hands.

After which he began to speak again of Mme. De Marbois. Claude listened attentively to him. Twelve o'clock struck, and still found him sitting there in a chair, stopping the conversation when a customer entered, resuming it as soon as he had gone;

"And you were saying?"

The old man went on with his story.

"If I may, I will come and see you sometimes, and we will talk about her," suggested the young man, as he rose.

"With pleasure, as often as you like."

And that is how they became great friends.

VII

OUT of the ten rooms in his house, Claude only occupied four, the drawing-room, the dining-room, the big bedroom, and a kind of office and library combined that smelt of moldy wood. And he very rarely entered that room, for the damp, speckled paper, and the dried flowers he had found between the leaves of a book, borrowed from the shelves, the last time he went in, had filled him with a strange feeling of depression.

The book was by de Maupassant. An ivy leaf marked the middle of the story, entitled *Apparition*. He began to read it.

As soon as he had read the first few words, the strangeness of the story piqued his curiosity. His was a soul that delighted in mystery, a mind ready to be seduced by the marvelous, and as soon as he read the description of the château, he noticed that it was strangely like his own house:

> The house seemed to have been abandoned for twenty years. In some extraordinary fashion, the gate, which was wide open and rotting away, still managed to stand upright. Weeds filled the paths, and hid the flower-beds on the lawn . . .

He stopped reading, and looked pensively out of the window, through the dust-encrusted panes. The garden was still the same as the day he had arrived, and he muttered:

"Strange! . . . anyone would think he had known Trois-Tourelles."

He went on reading:

> The room was so dark, that at first I could not make out anything. I stopped, struck by the moldy, sickly odor, as of rooms uninhabited, and condemned . . . dead rooms.

This time the feeling was so strong that he shut the book, and drew his hand across his brow. Urged on by a force, superior to his will, however, he opened it again, and went on reading, but with his nerves so much on edge that he ground his teeth, and although the day was cold and damp the perspiration trickled down between his shoulders.

> . . . At last, as my eyes had grown quite used to the darkness, I gave up all hope of seeing more clearly, and went to the writing-table. I seated myself, let down the flap, and opened the drawer of which I had been told. It was crammed full . . .

"Now then! Now then!" said Claude, aloud, "you are not going to let yourself be influenced by this sort of thing!"

He took the book, and put it back on the shelves, but, far from disappearing, the feeling of uneasiness became more pronounced. This unfamiliar house of his, where each wall seemed to shut in shadow and silence, disturbed him. A door, set in a corner, drew his attention, and he went up to it. He had hardly touched the handle, before it turned on its hinges, and the sour smell of a wine-cellar came straight at him, as though hunted forth by some underground breath.

He began to tremble. If there had not been the sound of cart-wheels on the road, he would not have dared to go in.

The window made a rectangular patch in the darkness. He opened it, and pushed back the shutters; the branches of the great cypress, fixed firmly against them, held them back. He took this to be a warning not to pursue his investigations any further, and drew away. But curiosity was stronger, and with his head full of the story he had just read, he went to the writing-table, and let down the flap.

A heap of different things lay there; empty cases, little cardboard boxes, letters thrown down every which way, and a few books. Already he was smiling at this fears, when at the back of the drawer, he found a packet, carefully tied up. It contained letters, a bunch of dead flowers, and a photograph.

"Some relation," thought he.

It was the portrait of a serious-looking man of about sixty, with a gentle, rather sad expression. He dived into his memory, but could not remember ever having seen the face, and yet he felt that it was not quite strange to him. On the other side of it was a date: August 9th, 1880 . . . and he was born on April, 1881. Measuring time by the length of his own life, he thought:

"How old it is!"

Upon which he put everything tidy again, and went back into the library to finish the story he had begun to read; the book, the title of which he had forgotten, could not be found anywhere.

This trifling incident made him think. Was it not the picture of his own life, this sudden glimpse of something, as bruskly removed from his sight? For the first time since his arrival, he was linking the present with the past, and less certainly than in Paris, but irritating, nevertheless, came the usual hesitation.

When night came, he ate his supper without appetite, and as soon as he had swallowed the last mouthful, returned to the library. But he fingered volume after volume in vain, searched all the shelves, tried to remember where he had put the book, but could not find it. He was getting angry, when Mère Chagne came in on tip-toe, and said:

"It is M. Coutelet who has come to call upon the master, if it does not disturb him!"

M. Coutelet! What did he want with him at that time of night?

He thrust back the books, dusted his hands, and replied:

"Very well, I will come . . . or stay . . . ask him if he will come up here . . ."

M. Coutelet apologized for coming out at such a late hour:

"If I am at all in your way, do not mind saying so. I was walking along, smoking my pipe, and, looking up, saw a light in your house, and rang the bell, just on chance . . ."

"You did very well," replied Claude; "do please sit down." The old man sat down in an armchair:

"It made me feel quite strange, seeing a light in this room."

"Why?" asked Claude.

"Because for twenty-five years the shutters have never been opened . . . I can understand that you like to sit in this room; books are the greatest friends a man can have, and if I had the good fortune to own such an extensive library, I should spend the whole of my time here. Your mother was very fond of this room; sometimes I used to come and chat with her here. I borrowed her books, and I believe I have read the greater part of them . . . Do you read much?"

"I? Very little . . . too little . . . but I'm going to get to work and will ask you to help me choose where to begin . . . Perhaps you can even do me a service now. Just imagine! half an hour ago I was reading a book. I had to go into another room, and replaced it on a shelf. Now I can't find it, and I am very interested in a story which I may never be able to finish . . . If only I remembered the title . . ."

"What was it about?"

"A story about . . ."

He related the first few pages. M. Coutelet interrupted him. "That is *Apparition* by de Maupassant, and the story is in the volume entitled *Clair de Lune*. It should be here."

He took the lamp, got on a stool and pointed to a row of books, glanced at several, and said:

"I don't see it; a book that is out of its place is as good as a book that is lost, but if you're anxious to hear the end, I can tell it to you."

Claude listened to him more and more attentively.

When he had finished, he remarked in a low voice, his chin in his hands:

"That's a strange adventure . . . and the sort of story I should write if I could write. I like tales of mystery, they respond to the thoughts that occupy my mind. I find in them points of contact with my deeper self. The mysterious attracts and terrifies me all at the same time; in spite of myself I seek it . . ."

"Heredity is a curious thing," mused M. Coutelet; "your poor mother liked that sort of book; and the last book I ever saw in her hands was the very one you cannot find."

"The fact that I glanced through it, might be a warning then, a word from Behind the Veil?" murmured Claude.

"I do not believe in the manifestation of immaterial forces," smiled the old man. "Once upon a time, I used to dabble in Spiritualism, and . . ."

He stopped. Claude looked him straight in the face:

"Go on . . ."

"And," went on M. Coutelet, in the tone of a man who regrets he has spoken lightly, "my opinion today is that there are things on which it is better not to dwell; it is only wise."

"Wisdom and truth are not always the same," objected Claude, "and I, who am only an ignorant, primitive fellow, am inclined to believe in a sort of fatal link, if the word does not displease you, used in this sense, between the fact that I chose the very book my mother loved to read, and the fact, guided by the hero of the story, I discovered in a room which otherwise I never should have entered, a writing-desk crammed full of letters, and the portrait of a man, whom I do not know, but whose face I swear is familiar to me . . ."

As he spoke he had gone to the inner room, had opened the writing-desk, and taken the photograph from the drawer. M. Coutlelet took it and looked at it, then at Claude, and gave it back without a word. His face wore a look of surprise, and his manner was a little nervous.

"Do you know who it is?" asked the young man.

"No..."

"Are you sure?"

"Is one ever sure of anything?" replied the old man.

The lamp, which stood on a little table, lighted up the carpet on the floor; in front of the two men the writing-desk gaped open, the curtains, black at the top, less soiled at the bottom, hung before the windows; a picture on the wall was crooked, and a thick spider's web was stretched across an angle, like a fragile nest.

"Is this not exactly the scene described in *Apparition*?" said Claude. "Does not this room strike you as uncanny? ... I hardly dare to raise my voice, and you, yourself..."

"How amusing," murmured M. Coutelet.

A smile curved Claude's lips:

"Come, M. Coutelet! Tell the truth; you know whose photograph that is. What's the good of denying it? I read faces better than books."

"As a matter of fact," replied the apothecary after a moment's hesitation, "that face is not unknown to me... I must have seen it long ago... but after all these years, it is impossible to tell you where and when..."

Claude lifted the lamp, and noticed his white face:

"My word, M. Coutelet! you would not tremble more if you saw a ghost!"

"There are no such things as ghosts," answered M. Coutelet, trying to laugh.

At the same moment, the light shone on the mirror, reflecting Claude's face.

"No, no," pronounced the old man with strange eagerness, "you must not believe in ghosts."

Claude looked at his reflection in the glass, then at the photograph, and murmured in a voice hoarse with feeling:

"Are you sure? . . . Tell me, is it this light or a tendency of my imagination to exaggerate things? . . . It seems to me that we are not two men here, but three, that the face I am looking at in the glass is not mine, and that it resembles the photograph . . ."

"Leave it be, leave it be," said M. Coutelet firmly, "you are the dupe of your imagination . . . How do you think there could be any such resemblance? . . . Come, let us go and have a smoke in the garden. The atmosphere of rooms long uninhabited is unhealthy in every respect. The fresh air will show you life as it really is and not as your novelists imagine it; and chance, which is responsible for many things, has not allowed you to find the de Maupassant book again. That sort of literature is bound to be bad for a bundle of nerves like you. I will find something better for you."

"Very well, let us look," said Claude, going towards the library.

"Later . . . some other time . . . tomorrow," proposed M. Coutelet.

"If I were as nervy as you say I am," said Claude, "do you not think I should see other reasons than a mere desire for the evening air, in your eagerness to leave this room?"

Then he blew out the lamp, moved aside to allow his guest to pass, shut the door, and locked it, and when they were on the stairs, continued:

"And, after all, it is only one more mystery . . . a little more shadow to follow other shadows . . ."

"It really grieves me to see you so upset," said M. Coutelet, as they reached the gate.

"Sooner or later, it had to come," answered Claude with sorrowful irony . . .

"As well as the fact that I was too happy in this village."

VIII

Claude pushed open the door of the chemist's shop, just as M. Coutelet was drawing the shutters to. It was night; the rain was sweeping over the houses, a gust of wind nearly threw the shutters against him.

"I don't want to find fault," cried M. Coutelet, "but you have fixed on a bad day to go out, and I was not expecting you in a gale. Take off your mackintosh. What a state you're in! Go on, I'll light the fire. Good Lord! Where have you been! You have cut yourself, you are hurt . . ."

"I? Where?"

"There . . ."

"No, I'm not," snapped Claude, "you know it's the color of my hands."

"I'd forgotten," confessed M. Coutelet without taking offense at the exasperated tone of his young friend.

Claude dropped into a chair, while the apothecary threw logs on the fire, and held out his hands to the flame:

"A glass of rum?" suggested M. Coutelet.

"No, thank you, I never touch spirits."

"Perhaps you're right; but you won't mind if I am less wise . . ."

He swallowed a mouthful, and sat down.

"Now, to what do I owe the pleasure of your visit?"

"You have no idea?"

"Not the least in the world . . ."

Claude looked at him, incredulous; he repeated:

"I assure you."

"I thought everybody knew already," said Claude. "Something . . . an incident happened this morning which is going to compel me to leave this place. I will tell you about it, frankly; promise that you will be frank with me."

"I promise you."

"You know little Marie Gravelot, the farmer's daughter? She is a nice little girl, gentle and intelligent, to put it plainly, she attracted and interested a lonely fellow like me. I sometimes went to find her in the meadows. We chattered and laughed. Now and again, I gave her a trifle to buy herself fineries. Well, this morning, maybe because these last few days I had felt so depressed, maybe because I liked her . . . I went near her . . . very near. She was not frightened."

"The girls of this canton are not over prone to timidity," remarked the old man, smiling.

"The fact remains," went on Claude, "that I was going to kiss her when, as I bent over her, I suddenly had the thought to put my fingers round her neck. She began to laugh and said: 'You aren't going to strangle me, Monsieur Claude?' And, urged on by some demon, I answered: 'Yes, I am.'"

"Of course, you were joking," cried M. Coutelet.

"Nothing of the kind. Any such thought was far from my mind. The words I said were the expression of my desire, and that is where the thing becomes incomprehensible. Unreasoning, calm, with a definite knowledge that I was about to kill, I began to press so hard that she pulled away from me, frightened. My fingers still gripped her . . . She threw herself backwards, and slipped so that, thank God, she twisted my arm, and I let her go. At once the fit of madness which had seized upon me vanished. I kneeled down beside her, not to harm, but to help her, as much troubled at her hurt as I was horrified by the attack, as though I had not been author of both. She got up, and, seeing me beside her, unable to guess at the mysterious upheaval that had taken place inside me, left her cattle and ran away. I followed her, so bewildered, so dazed that I did not know what I was doing, and passed her house without knowing it. Some women were gossiping on the doorstep; when they saw me they stopped talking; the child hid her face in her apron, but as I was passing the group, I heard her father growl:

"'He thinks they are all like his mother . . .'"

"I thought I should leap upon him. No doubt I ought to have done so. But my shame was so great, that I pretended I had not heard, and went on my way.

"Only, since then those words echo in my head, and I feel I shall never have any rest until they are explained . . . And I have come to you; you knew my mother . . . do you know what they mean?"

"Your mother was an admirable woman . . . gentle, charitable . . . and not very happy . . ."

"I know, I know . . . But the remark I quote refers to something else . . . It is not my mother's personality that I seek to know at this moment, but something of her life. If that man said such a thing lightly, he'd better look out for himself . . . Otherwise, I will go away, and no one will ever hear of me again . . . You see what your silence means."

"Are you going to treat a chance word, spoken in anger, so seriously?"

"Instead of trying to soothe me, give me an honest answer. I have been too long on the brink of my life's mystery to draw back the moment I see any chance of solving it . . . Besides it is no good arguing; either you will tell me, or I will force that rascal to do so; no matter to what lengths I have to go, I will get the truth out of him. Perhaps I may avoid some serious solution, some irreparable act, in coming thus to you . . . For I swear to you, M. Coutelet, that if I leave your house without learning anything, I will go through with this matter to the end! You understand what that means, and that no one can foresee how far threats will take a man like me."

He spoke with savage resolution, almost in a whisper, refusing to meet the other's eye. The apothecary felt that he meant what he said, and that if he wished to avoid trouble, he himself must now speak. He did so, sadly, and kindly, in the tone of a man whom age and experience have rendered indulgent:

"Faith! my dear fellow, you are putting me in a sad fix. Before condemning village gossip with the vehemence of a Parisian, you should realize that villagers judge the life of Paris with a somewhat primitive sternness . . . The people here learn morality at church; to them it is the same for everybody, as though life did not make a point of complicating everything, even morality, so much so that they can hardly forgive Our Lord for having defended the woman taken in adultery."

"So that was it!" cried Claude with his clenched hands on his mouth.

"No, no! Of course not! . . . I chose that example to make you see how much more difference there is than people think, between the mentality of country and town people. Your mother was a model wife."

"Well?"

"Peasant curiosity goes farther back than marriage. You and I only ask a woman to give an account of her life from the moment she takes a husband. They go deeper into the past, pick it to pieces, with a severity which is . . . oh! less wicked than childish . . . and consider as sinning what to us is mere incident . . ."

He stopped, hoping that Claude would not compel him to go into further details, but, buried deep in his armchair, his hands spread flat on his knees, Claude did not open his mouth. So he went on, correcting sentences and words, keeping back the revelation of truth.

"Suppose you married her; suppose you married a young girl? Everybody would want to know where she had lived before, who her parents were, and how they got their money. A widow? What her first husband had died of, and if she had been a good wife. A divorced woman? The reasons for divorce, and if the verdict were for or against her. A woman who was none of these things and had lived an independent life? . . ."

"I understand," said Claude slowly and distinctly . . . "My mother loved my father before she married him . . ."

M. Coutelet replied by a vague nod.

"Go on," Claude insisted, "there is something else, and you have told me too much not to tell me all."

"You are right," said the old man; "and you would make a mountain out of what is a very frequent thing. Your mother was poor. A friend bought the house where you live, and the farm around it, in order to provide for her . . . She lived an irreproachable life here. Occasionally the friend came to see her, and went away again. It was then that M. de Marbois knew her . . . loved her . . . and married her . . . You know enough of the peasants by now to realize how severely they would judge such a marriage . . . Now you know as much as I do."

"Just one more word. Was this friend ever heard of after my mother's marriage?"

"No. He died a short while before."

"Ah! exclaimed Claude. "Death certainly does arrange things well . . . but let us go on . . . So my mother was rich?"

"I don't know, my dear fellow, I really don't know," murmured M. Coutelet, visibly embarrassed.

"Let us go on then," said Claude, smiling, "and could you tell me . . . about . . . when the friend died?"

"The end of August or beginning of September, 1880."

"What a memory!" said Claude admiringly.

M. Coutelet bent down to take a log from his wood-chest; Claude watched him and went on:

"The death must have caused a deep impression on you, for you to remember the date so exactly, thirty years after."

"Sometimes one forgets important dates in one's own life, and remember the date of an incident that concerns someone else. For instance, I remember . . ."

"Don't trouble to tell me about things that I can very well conceive," said Claude.

"The fact is you are a terrible examining magistrate!" M. Coutelet tried to speak jokingly. "You turn my answers inside out."

He finished what was left in the glass beside him. With a hand on his shoulder, Claude pressed him into his chair again.

"Examining magistrate? What a word to use! . . . Yes, I am naturally curious, but haven't you repeatedly told me that in a small town people attach importance to small things? . . . Thus, perhaps, you could tell me, what the . . . friend . . . died of?"

M. Coutelet pushed back his chair, and rose, suddenly; then he sat down again, and replied:

"I don't know . . ."

"I should like to know," murmured Claude. "Would you believe it, when I heard the date of his death, and compared it with that of my birth . . ."

"What beastly weather!" complained M. Coutelet, going to the window. "Excuse me while I fasten the shutters; the wind will blow them away."

"Yes . . . yes . . . do!" answered Claude.

Then, as M. Coutelet came back to the fire, he went on in a careless tone:

"So you don't know what he died of?"

"I've no idea . . ."

"Did he not die here, then?"

"Yes," murmured the old man, more and more embarrassed.

"And no one sent for you, who knew my mother and were as good as any doctor in this village? Think, M. Coutelet, that we are confronted by facts now, which are easily verified, and that it would be absolutely useless to try and hide anything from me."

"As a matter of fact, my reticence was due to a desire not to worry you . . . The gentleman in question died of an accident . . . he was found one morning lying on the floor of the library . . . a blood clot probably . . ."

"Now we've come to it!" ejaculated Claude with a sigh.

"What did you say?"

"Nothing. Thank you for the information you have given me and which I will try to utilize. I feel better already for having spoken to you . . . But the rain is stopping, the wind too . . . I will go home again."

He slipped into his mackintosh, and, just as he was about to go, changed his mind, put a hand into his pocket, and took out a photograph which he showed to M. Coutelet.

"I showed it to you the other day, and you told me that you did not know who it was. But now, if you think a moment, is it not the portrait of that friend? . . ."

"Maybe," replied the apothecary.

Claude tried to laugh:

"How vague your memory has suddenly become, when it was so true a moment ago."

"I think perhaps it is the friend," said M. Coutelet.

He was meditating deeply.

"You wish to add something?" asked Claude.

"No . . . no . . . not at all."

"I thought perhaps you did . . . You looked so attentively, first at this and then at me . . . But there . . . I'm not surprised; I have looked often and long at that picture . . ."

Then, putting an end to the conversation, he opened the door and looked out into the night. It was pitch dark. The lamp which M. Coutelet sheltered with one hand, threw a circle of light on the road. Claude gnawed at his mustache, and could not make up his mind to go.

"If you're afraid you will not find your way," M. Coutelet proposed, "I have a spare room, and shall be only too delighted if you will use . . ."

"No, thank you . . . I must go home . . . I have work to do . . . things . . ."

He said the last words in a mysterious voice that made the old man uneasy.

"Nothing rash now," he said to him in a fatherly tone.

"Don't worry," Claude reassured him with a little laugh, "the time is not yet ripe."

IX

For ten days Claude never went outside the house. Convinced that the incident of little Marie had spread far and wide, he feared the peasants' attitude towards him.

In his own home even, Père and Mère Chagne only addressed him when they were obliged to, or at least that is how he looked at it. He felt a dumb hostility around him, that warned him of danger. Even close to the fire, the bitter cold made him shiver. He ate without appetite, and remained for hours at the window, watching for something, he knew not what, through the rain that fell incessantly. The sound of voices in the road, the scrunching of the gravel path, the tinkle of the door-bell, made his heart beat furiously, and filled him with a terror akin to that of the criminal who momentarily expects the arrival of the police. Winter, moreover, had entered the house and was settling in.

Long before nightfall, the branches of the cypress trees, which had not yet been pruned, drew a dark curtain before his windows. The cavern smell, which had upset him when he first came, and which had been dispersed by the summer sunshine, spread itself abroad again; here and there velvety patches of mildew, encircled with the damp, stained the wallpaper or spotted the sides of the pictures. Yet he had not made up his mind to go away, and with autumn hardly at an end, calculated how many months lay between it and spring, attaching a supernatural significance to his residence at Trois-Tourelles, fully convinced that Fate had given him this house for some mysterious purpose, and watching the hands of the clock go round as he listened to the drip of falling water.

On the fifth day, the postman rang at the gate. Claude pulled aside the curtain, and seeing the man slip something into the box, went downstairs. Mère Chagne was making for the door, but he stopped her:

"Do not trouble, I'll go."

The letter-box, from which the paint was peeling and which was all rusty inside, contained a packet of letters, tied together with string.

Newspapers for him, who took so little interest in the political, and for that matter, in every-day affairs? It struck him as comical, and thinking the postman had made a mistake, he went out on the pavement, and hailed him:

"Hi! *Mon vieux!* This isn't for me!"

The postman came back; while he was approaching, Claude read the address. Seeing his name, he corrected himself:

"I'm sorry, I made a mistake . . . it's for me all right."

"I was also thinking . . . !" grumbled the postman.

Claude cut the string and looked at the names; there were three copies of the *Echo Vendèen*. He thought to himself:

"They want me to take it in."

He glanced through the first page, and seeing nothing that interested him in the least, examined the wrapper.

The writing was unknown to him, exactly like any other business hand. He went into the library. The wood fire on the hearth was going out; he opened one of the papers, made a wad of it, set fire to it, and when it was nearly burnt and he could feel the heat of it on his finger-tips, he quickly pulled it from the fire again, and put it out under his foot.

At the bottom of the page was a paragraph, marked with a red X. No doubt, that was what the anonymous sender wished him to read. So he read it . . . As he did so, drops of perspiration stood out upon his face.

Saint-Fulgent, 12 August

Yesterday morning, M. Deguy, who was staying at his country house, Trois-Tourelles, was found dead in his library. The deceased was clad in trousers, a nightshirt, a dressing-gown and slippers, like a man preparing to go to bed. There was a certain amount of disorder in the room, but the body showed no marks of violence. The fact that there was an open book on the floor leads to the belief that death, due, either to a sudden blood clot or the rupture of a blood-vessel, was sudden, and this would explain why Mlle. Colette Fagant, a young artist, with whom M. Deguy had been staying for three days, heard nothing in the next room where she was sleeping. In spite of this the court has refused permission to bury the body, and an inquest will be held.

Claude brushed his hand across his brow and looked round him. In this room, perhaps in the very spot where he was sitting a man had died.

It never occurred to him that the article merely repeated what the apothecary had already told him. In print, the words had a harsher meaning, and several times he repeated his mother's maiden name: Colette Fagant. He thought it pretty and pathetic, like everything that had to do with her, telling himself that he would rather it were his than de Marbois, which though finer-sounding, and more aristocratic, was brutal and proud.

The fire which had flamed up for a moment went out again; bits of charred wood fell from the logs with a sharp crackle. Shadows were already gathering in the corners, blotting out the contents of the room. The words in the paper he held open before him ran into one another; he took another, unfolded it, and seeing nothing but a jumble of words, made up his mind that the fact of his not being able to see to read was a warning to seek no further . . . However, he lit his lamp, so that the light should banish all the fancies that assailed him. But so far from bringing him respite, the light only gave a more definite turn to his thoughts. The words of the article were clear in his memory, and he conjured up in his mind the finding of the body lying across the floor. The room was probably in the same state then as it was today, and its disorder made the vision more clear. Since his visit to M. Coutelet, he had not quitted it. Pacing up and down between the four walls, moving one thing, pushing back a chair or tables, sleeping half the night on the couch, even eating on a corner of the table, without giving Mère Chagne a chance to sweep.

The night before, as he had not been able to sleep, he had read or tried to read, rummaging around among the books, trying to fix his attention on lines that slid away under his eyes, without leaving the least memory behind them, and, finally, putting the volumes back as fast as they bored him.

A great weariness made him want to lie down, a feeling of desperate loneliness made him afraid to sleep, a sleep that was sure to be heavy and haunted by bad dreams; but above all curiosity to see what the other two papers contained, kept him awake . . .

So, he took the second copy, dated September 3rd, and his eyes fell upon the same red-penciled cross that had drawn his attention to the first article. The heading was in large letters:

THE MYSTERY OF TROIS-TOURELLES

What we drew attention to in our edition of August 18th as "miscellaneous news" is assuming the proportions of a mysterious occurrence. The autopsy on the body of M. Deguy, as ordered by the court, has given no result. We believe we are right, however, in saying that the magistrates have not abandoned the idea of murder, and strange rumors are circulating in the country-side.

We transcribe these merely as information, and not in any way do we lay claim to any one of the somewhat contradictory opinions. In any case, the inquiries which our correspondent is making on the spot are sufficient to vouch for a certain number of rather disturbing facts.

The house which goes by the name of Trois-Tourelles, and formerly belonged to the Comtes de Chenaille, was purchased two years ago under the name of Mlle. Colette Fagant. The papers drawn up by Maitre Bouzot, a notary at Montaigu, are in order, and the validity of the title-deeds needs nothing to be desired. But as the family of Mlle. Fagant is very poor, and she herself has no fortune, it seemed to us very interesting to find out by what intermediary the purchase was effected. Now it turns out that the purchaser was M. Deguy, and we are betraying no secret when we say he was looked upon as a *very intimate friend* of the young lady, by the people of those parts.

What is more, they observed the utmost discretion in their relations to one another. M. Deguy came only very rarely to the house, and the occasions on which he stayed there were even rarer. It was his custom to call in on his way elsewhere, and to treat his hostess with a great and fatherly respect. Sometimes, too, Mlle. Fagant went away, and joined him either at Nantes in the winter, or at Guérande in the summer.

Latterly, a project of marriage between them had been touched upon, and a will drawn up by M. Deguy that left all his fortune to his young friend.

Now people say, and we repeat these rumors with the utmost reserve, that in the meanwhile Mlle. Fagant had made the acquaintance of a young man of noble family, but poor; that this young man had come secretly at least once to Trois-Tourelles, and that, having heard of it, M. Deguy had threatened to destroy the will and to give up all idea of marriage.

The police are on the track of this person, and do not despair of finding him; we shall help them to do so, as far as lies within our power.

Claude let the paper drop; at a distance of thirty years, these details were full of strange significance. The veil, which until that moment had hidden his mother's past, was torn in twain, and at the same moment a terrible question rose up to confront him: he asked himself without daring a reply, who was the young man of noble family, who had been seen in the village, and whose share in all of this seemed so strange.

He remembered the disparaging way in which his father spoke of "little provincial papers, full of venom and wickedness." These articles certainly aimed at impartiality, and these were careful not to overstep the limits of mere information, but with what cruelty they inquired into the private life of his mother and with what malicious joy the country-people must have passed the papers round at that time, and read them aloud in the evenings, sitting around the fire.

He took up the third sheet. The same heading, *The Mystery of Trois-Tourelles*, sprawled across the front page. But, if in the preceding articles the tone had been calm, in this one, it became threatening:

> The case of which during four weeks Mlle. Colette Fagant has been the heroine, is legally speaking at an end. What we mean by that is that the law no longer mentions it. But we, as impartial agents, have the right to pursue an inquiry, which public feeling demands. It is to everyone's advantage that full light should be thrown on such a case. The identity of the mysterious X who went, secretly, once at any rate, to the château has not yet been discovered. Does that signify that X only exists in the imagination of the village folk? As far as we are concerned, the answer is not doubtful. The examination was closed at the very moment when people were beginning to talk, and the inquiries were carried out with the most disconcerting nonchalance. Who can say whether a more careful search in the old house, with its many nooks and crannies, would not have yielded unexpected results? Today, the tendency is to rely on chance alone, that great ally of examining magistrates; and is not that too simple a method, when we are concerned with the death of a man? . . . And if, as we should prefer to believe, no crime was committed, should not those whom public opinion suspects, be declared innocent in

such a fashion, that they themselves could have the law on persons who, not later than yesterday, removed a wreath which had been placed upon the dead man's grave?

Two cuttings were pinned to the last paper. One said:

> We are informed of the marriage of M. Marcel de Marbois, and Mlle. Colette Fagant.

The other:

> The Comtesse de Marbois has given birth to a son, Claude.

The same hand which had penned the address on the wrapper had added two dates: October 7th, 1880, on the first cutting, and April 12th, 1881, on the second.

A sound made Claude start, and he drew his attention from the amazement with which the papers filled him. He looked round the room and saw that a book which he had placed on the shelf the night before had fallen on the carpet. He picked it up, looked at it, turned it over, and seeing that it was open at the story, *Apparition*, uttered a cry, and flung it far from him, in terror.

X

DAWN was near, and Claude still searched the drawers in the bedroom. The discovery of the book, which for so long he had been unable to find, at the very moment when certain suspicions that he had not dared to formulate, were materializing, had thrown him into a state of excitement which verged on madness . . .

Madness traversed by lucid flashes, in which his thoughts linked themselves together, only to fall back into a chaos of anger and doubt, to come up against the loss of memory, to visions of inconceivable violence, which he thrust aside with savage energy, and recalled with childish weakness.

When exhaustion came, and his arms hung limp, his fingers were covered with greasy dust, his lips dry, his eyelids twitching, he egged himself on by word and gesture:

"Seek! Seek! Perhaps the truth is there!" . . .

Around him, linen, ribbons, and papers lay scattered. At first his hands felt about, turning the contents of the drawer upside down, then he put everything in order, stopping now and then to glance pityingly at an account book, containing his mother's entries, or a bit of lace, to which he insisted a faint perfume still clung, in spite of the years. Then his anger melted into infinite regret, for the love that he had never been able to give or receive.

"If I have to spend my days and nights in turning everything over, to pull this house to pieces, brick by brick, to dig up the garden, and drain the lake, I will end by knowing."

When he had emptied every drawer in the writing-table, he slipped his hand between the two supports, and drew out a little note-book which had fallen down behind, and which he opened in rather a perfunctory fashion. What chance was there that he would find a slip of paper or a note inside? His surprise was all the greater, therefore, to find a telegram addressed to C.F. poste restante, Nantes. It was stamped August 12, 1880, and in Paris, and said:

Shall arrive tonight. Marcel.

He closed his eyes, and fell into a chair.

It was Sunday. On the stroke of nine, he heard Mère Chagne talking in the passage with somebody.

"If he is asleep, don't disturb him," said a voice.

"He must be surely up by now," answered the woman, "that is, if he went to bed."

The door opened gently; Claude turned his head, and looked pensively at Mère Chagne, and M. Coutelet, who was behind her.

"I told you so!" grumbled the farmer's wife, "he spends whole nights like that! . . . And during the day he stays as he is now, or with his nose glued to the window, taking no more notice of people than if they were talking double-Dutch."

M. Coutelet nodded his head.

"Not to mention the fact that he will be ill," went on the good woman.

She went forward softly and called: "Are you wanting anything now, master?"

Claude turned his head away and looked towards the window. The old woman sighed and said confidentially: "Like his mother . . . as like as two peas. You speak to him, perhaps he will listen to you . . ."

M. Coutelet went up to Claude, put a hand on his shoulder, and remarked cheerfully: "Up already and at work?"

The lamp was going out with a smell of oil and smoke. The daylight crept waveringly through the shutters. Claude had not moved. The apothecary opened the window, pushed back the shutters and, pointing to the sky, which was flecked with white clouds, went on: "No one should stay in on such a day! As for me, I've shut up shop; people must not be ill on Sunday, and I'm going for a walk in the woods. Will you come?"

The only answer Claude made was to cover his eyes with his hand as though the light hurt them. M. Coutelet drew the curtains, and the room was again in darkness. Mère Chagne, who could not understand anyone remaining silent when spoken to, repeated her question:

"Are you wanting anything now, master?"

Claude sighed, and stretched himself, pressing his shoulders against the back of the chair, and replied:

"No, thank you, you may leave us."

He waited until she shut the door, and the noise of her footsteps had died away in the passage, and only then did he turn to M. Coutelet.

His face was drawn with fatigue, his cheeks were covered with black marks where his fingers had rested, his eyelids lifted and drooped again, slowly.

"Come," said M. Coutelet, "what is the matter? It is surely not the incident with the child that has upset you to this extent? It has long been forgotten . . . The father made a fuss for the sake of appearances . . . All you have to do is make him a present of a quarter's rent."

"He hates me, and has reason to hate me," said Claude with bent head.

"Good heavens, my dear fellow! As if the parents in this part of the country were compelled to hate every young man who hugged their daughters too closely! Do you forget that we are only a short distance from the Marais? You don't look as though that meant anything to you? Well, on the day of the fair, at the Marais, the girls and boys may do anything they like . . . anything except . . . Anyway, that leaves a pretty good margin, don't you think? . . . Ah! these old customs!"

And as he knew all the ways and manners of the countryside, partly for the pleasure of telling it, and partly to make his friend think of other things, he began to describe the appearance of the public room in the inns on fair day; where couples sat on benches lined against the walls, and, without caring who saw them, shamelessly amused themselves in a thousand different ways, which were anything but guileless. With the racy description, he mingled a knowledge of legend, medical terms, and the easy indulgence of an old fellow, who can talk on any and every subject with absolute unconcern.

Claude smoothed out the creases in the carpet with the point of his shoe, so deep in his thoughts that the apothecary's voice sounded like a humming in his ears.

"That is what is called the Maréchinage," finished the old man. "Is it not a curious custom?"

Claude rose, went to the door, looked carefully to see that it was shut, and standing facing M. Coutelet, asked point blank:

"What sort of man was M. DeGuy?"

"M. DeGuy?" . . . repeated the apothecary, "M. DeGuy?"

"Yes, M. DeGuy who was found dead here on August 13th, 1880." His finger pointed to the floor in front of the bookcase.

"You know?" said the apothecary with an effort.

Claude merely replied: "What do you think!" and shrugged his shoulders. Then, as M. Coutelet said no more, he added:

"You see, nothing is hidden from me, nothing can be hidden from me."

He walked rapidly up and down the room.

By degrees, his voice grew calmer, more gentle:

"It is a strange story, certainly, that of the poor man, who was so good, so generous, dying here, without being able to call for help. But, as a matter of fact, why did you not tell me his name the other day."

M. Coutelet shook his head vaguely. Claude smiled.

"After all your secrets are your own, or perhaps I should say your reasons are your own."

"What possible reason could I have for concealing a detail that happened so long ago, and is of so little interest?" asked M. Coutelet.

"Do you really think it is of so little interest?"

"Really, I . . ."

"Very well . . . we will not speak of it again . . . But how pale you are now."

"I?"

"I imagined you were, but I must be making another mistake," replied Claude carelessly. "Is it loneliness, the depressing atmosphere of this house, the odor of ancient things that surrounds me, or only the desire for the supernatural, that has obsessed me these last days? . . . My senses, unless it be my imagination, are growing curiously alert, and show me things that I never dreamed of . . ."

"Hallucinations caused by nervous strain," explained M. Coutelet.

"It must be something of the kind," agreed Claude. "For instance, this portrait . . ."

He took from the mantelpiece the photograph he had found in the drawer, lifting it for the apothecary to see:

". . . Yesterday morning, when I was looking at it, I had an extraordinary feeling. Would you believe that when I looked first at this face, then my own in the mirror, it struck me there was a remarkable resemblance between the two; the same slanting eyes, the same bushy eyebrows, the same high-bridged nose, the same shaped chin, hair growing the same way, ears straight and flat at the top, and with the lobes adhering . . . I was extremely struck by it . . ."

"Fancy!" murmured M. Coutelet.

"Do you think so? Then my brain must be very disturbed, or very stubborn," he pronounced the last words with a sneer, "for at this very moment, I can see the same resemblance. Come, tell me, is it possible for one to delude oneself so greatly? . . . You who are a strong-minded man, and not a nervous wretch like me, you compare them . . . Dark is it? . . . That's soon remedied."

He went to the window, drew the curtains, came back holding the photograph in the tips of his fingers, and stood in three-quarter profile to the apothecary:

M. Coutelet turned away his head:

"Let that be, my dear fellow; throw that photograph in the fire . . ."

Claude clasped it to his breast:

"Throw it in the fire? . . . You can't mean that! . . . You cannot imagine how I prize it. It is such a weird feeling to see myself as I shall be thirty years hence. But I realize that all this is only perceptible to myself, and, after all, what can it matter as I'm the only one interested in this fact! And if I'm the sport of fancy, as you say, I intend to stick to it."

He replaced the photograph on the mantelpiece, beside the clock, looked at it, looked at himself in the glass, and repeated:

"In any case, it is a strange fancy . . ."

He rubbed his hands together, and laughed like a man pleased with his joke.

A ray of sunshine lighted up the library; M. Coutelet took advantage of it to say:

"Do come out with me: the country is beautiful, and it will be pleasant to chat as we walk along."

Claude shook his head:

"I cannot bring myself to leave this house; it contains more than the whole world for me. If I could tell you all it has taught me, you would be amazed. The silence is full of voices, the darkness of pictures, and to him who knows how to obey them, they reveal prodigious secrets. But what am I telling you, you who are a materialist? You do not believe in the survival of the soul, nor in the invisible worlds that surround you. It surprises you to see that I know so much, for you have looked upon me as a mere schoolboy until now. Science, faith, and truth, reveal themselves to whom they choose, and sometimes the forces Behind the Veil try their powers on the most humble. I should amaze you were I tell you one quarter of what I have learned these past five days. Perhaps I will tell you when the moment comes . . . Then . . ."

He spoke in the voice of a prophet, with radiant face and sweeping gestures. Suddenly he struck his forehead:

"But I have not told you the queerest thing of all! You remember de Maupassant's book, that we looked for in vain one afternoon? Well, my dear M. Coutelet, there it is at your feet, in front of you! I do not flatter myself that I found it; it came to find me . . . and I may say that it came at the given moment . . . Its disappearance was strange enough, but what name shall we give to its return?"

"Chance!" replied the old man.

"No!" said Claude sharply, "there is no such thing as chance; that is a word invented by man to hide his incapacity and failure to understand anything that lies beyond his scope. Chance does not exist, but hidden forces do; for everything is linked up. Nothing happens, however slight, futile, or fortuitous, which is not at the same time a consequence and a cause. Only nobody pays any attention to it! And so those, who like myself have been granted the gift of meditation, of reflection and deep thought during several days, so far removed from the world, that, as far as they are concerned, the present no longer exists, are looked upon as madmen, so lucid and reasonable have their minds become! . . . M. de Marbois had not waited my discovery of this intellectual retreat to give me the reputation of a lunatic. Would you believe it, one day, a few months ago, he wanted to send me to a madhouse? Oh, perhaps he was not altogether wrong, I am dangerous, very dangerous . . . Only it is not my fault . . . It is certain that sometimes my inmost thoughts are strangely cruel . . . That child Marie . . . well, I swear to you, my good sir, that I very nearly strangled her . . . At this moment, such an act seems monstrous to me; but I am quite unable to guarantee the next."

He opened his hands wide, and an expression of intense cruelty came on his face. Then at once the strained look left his face, a flush crept to his cheeks, and he went on in an ordinary voice:

"You are a delightful friend, M. Coutelet, and, what is more, a really learned man. What a pity that you came and buried yourself in such a hole! If I had time and strength, I should ask you to teach me hundreds of things . . . you have read and studied and remembered so much! . . . The nervous fits that take possession of me are perhaps caused by irritation at knowing nothing, or so little . . . Have you noticed that children are subject to fits of passionate temper that do not affect older people? Sometimes I think I have discovered a cure for my malady, a cure unsuspected by the greatest doctor, and at which, no doubt, he would laugh: study. Not the dry study of books, but the study of life . . . I think experimental science is marvelous. To me the most elementary explanations of the simplest phenomena are soothing. I tell you what, I will go out with you. As we go along, I will ask you about Nature and animals, and plants . . . I still think of the wonderful account you gave me in explanation of wireless telegraphy and electrical waves; and the other about the production of double, and triple and quadruple flowers . . ."

He rammed his hat on his head and, kicking away the things scattered about him, said, as he opened the door:

"Go first, M. Coutelet, I am with you."

"Like that?" cried the apothecary astonished . . . "Make yourself a little bit tidier, at least . . ."

"I don't attach any importance to my rag of a body," said Claude jokingly, "but if you really mind . . ."

He seized the water-jug that stood on the table, emptied it into the basin, which he finished filling with the contents of a dirty jar. The water was rusty. He dipped the end of a towel in it, and said as he held it to his face:

"How long has that water been here? Fifteen years? twenty perhaps? . . . When I think of that, I have no wish to use it; absurd, isn't it? Water is never anything but water . . . Still, I want fresh water, water drawn on purpose for me . . . This, here . . . Madame Chagne, bring me up a pail of water!"

As soon as it came, he turned up his sleeves, opened his shirt collar, and, without troubling to empty it into the basin, plunged his face into it, rubbing his neck and cheeks, dipping his head right in with exclamations of cold and delight. Then he turned down his sleeves, parted his hair with a comb, put on a tie, and asked gaily:

"How will that do?"

"Splendid," answered M. Coutelet.

Claude returned to the mirror, looked at himself complacently and remarked:

"It'll do, it'll do!"

His somber mood had left him, his movements were natural, and his voice cheerful. M. Coutelet rejoiced at the change.

"You see," he remarked, wishing to point out a moral, "man is not made for solitude, the best-balanced people get nervy and inclined to make much of their grievances, when they are lonely; the smallest worry takes on the proportions of a calamity, and, the shadow which blots out the design . . ."

"Don't speak of that again," cried Claude; "from today, I want to become a different man, I want to learn things . . . If it doesn't bore you too much, you shall be my teacher . . ."

"With pleasure."

"Perhaps I shall be a tiresome pupil. I may ask you all sorts of questions about all sorts of things, like a child. A child's questions are sometimes tiresome, embarrassing, unexpected . . ."

"I will do my best to answer them."

"To begin with, I will ask you one that has worried me for a long time . . ."

He pointed to the red stain that marked his two hands:

"What do you call that?"

"A *nævus* (from the mother), probably."

"And that means?"

"A mark which the child has on its body when it is born."

"And the reason?"

"A congenital deficiency in the production of a pigmentary matter . . ."

"That's no explanation; at the best it is a definition."

"If we attempt to solve the mystery of the formation of the human being, where will it lead us? . . . Science holds back; some worthy people, more simple-minded than savants, attribute these little defects to longings. For instance, if a child has a strawberry mark on some part of his body, they say his mother had an unsatisfied longing for strawberries during her pregnancy; when another has a mark that looks like a mouse, they say that a mouse frightened his mother before he was born. In your case, married women would say that your mother had a longing for wine . . ."

"It looks more like blood than wine," remarked Claude.

"Pooh! blood or wine it is only an old wife's tale . . ."

"Do you think it wise to make fun of that kind of thing? I have heard it said that popular beliefs often have a grain of truth in them . . . Did not you yourself tell me, the day we met an idiot child, that his mother had had a terrible fright before he was born?"

"That's true, I remember."

"Well, then?"

"The scientist, who makes no assertion without proof, does not, on principle, permit himself to deny anything, and, as we have no positive solution of this phenomenon, I grant you that any explanation is permissible."

"Ah!" Claude ejaculated, throwing his hat on the table.

His face had grown serious again; he sat down and began to think.

"Let us go out," said M. Coutelet.

Claude shook his head.

". . . And I who thought you so reasonable, and was going to give you such interesting lessons! You really must have a little more sequence in your ideas."

"You cannot imagine how tremendously they are in sequence," answered Claude.

"It doesn't look much like it."

"That's because you cannot read . . . nor can anybody for the matter of that . . . what is going on here," said he, touching his forehead.

Then, he lay back, his hands shading his eyes.

Now and again his lips moved.

M. Coutelet looked at him, sadly.

"Of what are you thinking?"

"I am thinking," replied Claude, "that this room, these books, the water that lay at the bottom of the jugs . . . everything that surrounds us, that we think dead, and which is only pretending . . . have seen strange happenings perhaps. I must question them again, I am sure they will speak to me . . . Besides, they have already begun to . . . Only nobody must come between us . . . When they have given up their secrets to me, I will let you know. Oh! it will not take long; now that I am on the right track, two or three days will surely suffice. Look, come here . . . Don't you see? . . . those papers quivering! . . . those pages moving?"

"It's the wind," murmured M. Coutelet, hoarsely.

"The wind? Do you really think so? I know it's their way of showing me they are here . . . Listen, did you hear that?"

"The wood of an old piece of furniture cracking."

Claude shrugged his shoulders.

"No! No! *They want to speak to me.* Generally these phenomena take place at night only. It must be something very urgent for them to speak like this, in broad daylight."

M. Coutelet stared at him, utterly amazed. Claude took no notice of his surprise, and, leading him to the door, he murmured with affectionate politeness:

"You will excuse me, won't you? . . . But it would rude of me to keep the Spirits waiting, and I think I should be mad not to take advantage of their services . . ."

"I will leave you," said M. Coutelet with a sigh.

Claude listened to his retreating footsteps and, holding the curtain aside, watched him depart. When he reached the yard, M. Coutelet beckoned to Mère Chagne. In order to hear what they were saying, Claude went into a little dressing-room, the dormer window of which was wide open, and stood with his ear glued to it, listening.

"How did you find him?" asked the farmer's wife. "Come, tell me, is he or is he not in his right senses?"

"He is peculiar, undoubtedly," answered M. Coutelet.

"If there were any likelihood of it going on, Chagne and I would rather leave. The other night he was calling and crying like a child; it made me feel frightened and sorry at the same time. Who knows what he might do at such moments?"

M. Coutelet scratched his head:

"For the time being, I do not think there is any danger. Content yourself with watching him, without letting him see it, and in case of need, let me know. In the meanwhile I am going to send a telegram to M. de Marbois. He will come and decide what shall be done. It is a matter of thirty-six or forty-eight hours' patience!"

"If that's the case . . . very well. Otherwise . . ."

Claude went back into his room, and rubbed his hands:

"Excellent, M. Coutelet."

XI

CLAUDE was sitting in the office on the ground-floor, when Mère Chagne opened the door and announced:
"Visitors for you, Monsieur Claude."
M. de Marbois entered at the same moment:
"Good-day, my boy."
"Good-day, monsieur," replied Claude.
M. de Marbois looked round at M. Coutelet who was behind him, and held out a hand to his son. But Claude pretended not to see, and merely pointed to a chair.
M. Coutelet had warned M. de Marbois that his son was in an extremely excitable state, and that he must not be surprised at anything peculiar in his conversation. He had put him on his guard against any possible gentleness that might precede extraordinary fits of fury in these words:
"It may be that when you first see him you will notice nothing of the condition that worries me; that M. Claude will give you the impression of absolute mental balance. If this should happen, do not imagine that I have been unnecessarily alarmed. Everything may change from one minute to another, and I, who have watched him closely, must confess, I find it quite impossible to tell you what words to choose, or what to abstain from, in order to provoke one of these attacks."

Nevertheless, he was amazed at his reception, and explained his visit haltingly:

"Just imagine! a short while since I was just about to put up my shutters, when, to my surprise, I saw your father! . . ."

"Yes," went on M. de Marbois, "I was worried at having no news of you, so I decided to come and see for myself."

"That is very kind of you . . . Besides, you have not taken me by surprise," answered Claude. "I am always ready for anything and was expecting your visit . . . But never mind that, the chief thing is that you are here."

He said these words with a courtesy that constrasted with his former brusk manner. M. Coutelet saw in this a sign of what he had mentioned to M. de Marbois as they went upstairs; this change of front was well timed to add something to his diagnosis, and throw light upon it. M. de Marbois glanced at him to show that he understood, and put in his word:

"How are you?"

"Very well; I've never been better. M. Coutelet will tell you, if he has not already done so, that I am in the best of health, and the country suits me wonderfully well. The house is charming, and the only thing that surprises me is that you have never thought of coming here for the holidays. When I arrived it was rather depressing, but I am having it put in order, and when the work I have decided upon is finished, it will be a very presentable place."

"Quite so!" M. de Marbois assured him, "but as it is now, it doesn't look very comfortable to me, and until the repairs are completed what do you say to a little voyage? M. Coutelet and I were discussing it as we came along."

"We'll see . . . yet I like it here. What is wanting? What do I need that I cannot get here?"

"It is not a case of starting at once," M. de Marbois corrected him.

"Autumn is pleasant in this part of the country," put in the apothecary.

"No doubt, no doubt," said Claude approvingly, "time enough for all that."

Then, suddenly, his easy attitude stiffened, he became ceremonious, and added graciously:

"I hope you will do me the honor of dining with me?"

The question seemed so out-of-place, that M. de Marbois was on the point of bursting out laughing. A father who has spent twelve hours in the train, to go and see his son, would generally consider such an invitation superfluous. A sign from M. Coutelet stopped him, and he replied in the same tone:

"Thank you, with the greatest pleasure."

At once Claude clapped his hands:

"That is nice of you, and gives me pleasure! Hurrah for light and gaiety! You are right, M. Coutelet, absolutely right! Life is good!"

He laughed. Mère Chagne who was standing on the threshold, stared in astonishment. He took hold of her arm:

"Mère Chagne, set three places, and give us some good wine."

She looked at him in amazement; her bewilderment amused him.

"You can't get over my being so gay? Try to imagine, my good woman, the joy that fills a person when those he loves best come to see him; a friend, who sometimes forsakes him . . . I am speaking to you, M. Coutelet . . ."

"Forgive me," stammered the apothecary, "I've been so busy these last few days . . ."

Claude patted the old man's wrist in friendly fashion:

"Of course, of course I understand . . ."

Then, open-armed, he turned to M. de Marbois:

"And a father . . ."

M. de Marbois stepped forward and opened his arms too; but already Claude had dropped his, and, seizing Mère Chagne by the shoulder, he shook her, crying:

"Yes, good dame! the best wine, the most delicious food! Ransack the cupboards, plunder the sideboards, hunt out the finest linen, the costliest silver!"

He pushed her out on the landing, and turning to his father said:

"It is my intention to treat you as well as I can, so that you may always remember my rustic hospitality."

When dinner was served they all sat down. Claude's appetite was excellent. He laughed, chatted, looked after his guests, like a host who knows his duties, and rejoices in them. Now and then, M. de Marbois looked first at his son, then at M. Coutelet, as much as to say to the latter:

"What have you been talking about? I think he is extremely sensible."

And M. Coutelet pursed up his lips in a way that meant: "Patience, you will see . . ."

As for Claude he took no notice of this mute interchange of opinion, but, glass in hand, said jokingly:

"Aren't you going to drink anything then?"

Presently, he stretched out a hand, and took a dusty bottle. Uncorking it carefully, he announced:

"Château-Laroze, 1880! That year, it appears, was an extraordinary one in every way. This wine is a few months older than I. The grapes from which it was pressed were ripening, when what was to be myself was just beginning to develop."

"No, thank you," said M. de Marbois, putting a hand over his glass.

"Don't you care for this brand?" cried Claude in astonishment. "I'm very sorry because I particularly thought you would like it. Perhaps, after all, it is not so good as I hoped . . . What is your opinion, M. Coutelet?"

"I think it is extremely good."

"If you don't care for the date," said Claude pleasantly to his father, "I can give you another . . . Here's some '79, and some '81. If I made a point of choosing that special year, it was because I thought you would be pleased with the attention; the date of the birth of an only son, is such an important one to parents!"

He remained with his arm extended, holding the bottle ready to pour.

"I am not thirsty now," protested M. de Marbois with a touch of impatience.

Claude bowed, and spoke of other things, so easily, and with such shrewd wit, that at last M. Coutelet unconstrainedly gave himself up to the enjoyment following on a good dinner well digested.

When the meal was ended they smoked and drank liqueurs, as they chatted about all kinds of things.

The clock struck eleven.

"An unheard-of time for the country!" remarked M. Coutelet as he put on his overcoat.

Claude accompanied him to the gate. The village was deserted; not a light in the windows, and the road shining white in the moonlight.

As he said au revoir to him, Claude retained M. Coutelet's hand in his:

"What are you thinking of?" asked the old man.

"I am thinking . . ." said Claude distinctly in a deep voice.

But, playing with the little flap of the letter-box, he added:

"I am thinking of nothing, of absolutely nothing . . ."

M. Coutelet took his departure. As he was about to step into the lane, he turned round. Claude had not moved. His shadow, which was gathered in a heap at his feet, looked like a pedestal making him appear taller.

"Good night," cried the apothecary.

"I will do my best," answered Claude.

Then, waiting till he had disappeared behind the wall, he looked carefully, and went back to his father. As he stood facing him, his face twitched slightly, but only for a moment, and he said:

"Allow me to take you to your room."

"I can go quite well by myself," answered M. de Marbois.

"What an idea!" said Claude. "I know my duty, and I have given orders for the bedroom on the first floor, near the library to be prepared for you . . . *my mother's room* . . . You don't seem to like the arrangement?"

"I?" ejaculated M. de Marbois, with the vivacity of a man surprised in the middle of his thoughts. "On the contrary . . . Although it is painful to be in a room once occupied by one who is no more . . ."

"Who is no more . . . who is no more . . . ? Do you really believe that human beings disappear so utterly and entirely?"

"What do you mean?" demanded M. de Marbois.

"I was just expressing a thought which is familiar to me, a thought which may be absurd . . . But please go first, and do not take any notice of my remarks."

They went upstairs. Claude went first, carrying a candle which he lifted high above his head, throwing dancing shadows on the walls. The stairs creaked continuously beneath their footsteps; M. de Marbois nearly stopped; Claude explained that the old wood was still warping, or that the worms were accomplishing their work of patient destruction.

"And yet," said he, as they reached the landing, "there are times when I cannot believe that there is nothing else in the cry of inanimate objects than the mere movement of matter. For instance, this library . . ."

He pushed open the door and drew back before his father.

M. de Marbois hesitated a moment on the threshold.

"You still feel the same sadness in being where people died?" murmured Claude.

M. de Marbois straightened himself, and went in.

Claude had already forgotten his remark, and was pursuing the same idea he had expressed a few seconds before:

"I was saying that I think there is more in the cry of inanimate things than the mere movement of matter. On several occasions, in this room particularly, I have been able to vouch for one strange phenomenon; that bookcase which remains silent when M. Coutelet or Mère Chagne are present, begins to creak the moment I go near it *alone*."

M. de Marbois shrugged his shoulders.

"Oh, I know," Claude agreed, "it may sound peculiar. People usually have a contempt for what they have not learned by routine, and with the passion that men have for denying, instead of seeking knowledge, the cleverest among them turn round and round in the miserable little circle they call fact; and it is very flat and arid ground, like that of a threshing-floor; in both instances, there is not enough fresh soil to nourish the forgotten seed. Deny that if you feel brave enough."

"At the present moment, what I feel most is a great desire to sleep," answered M. de Marbois.

"I should be grieved to deprive you of one moment's sleep," Claude assured him, "and I admire the light-hearted way in which you can put aside thoughts like these, which stir me so deeply. Shall I make a confession? Sometimes I have been afraid in this room."

"Poor Claude," said M. de Marbois, smiling, "afraid, and of what?"

"If people knew what they were afraid of, they would not be afraid. I speak for myself of course. Doubtless you have never experienced the feeling."

"Never."

"I envy you. Some evenings I have to exert uncommon will-power to make myself stay in this room; but I must add that now I come in here without the least fear. But, upon my word; there's something uncanny about that! Do you hear?"

"I hear nothing."

"You will hear," murmured Claude, raising his fingers; "and now? can you not hear the bookcase creaking? Once . . . twice . . . three times . . ."

"When you walk about near old furniture," M. de Marbois explained. "Give me my candlestick."

"Old furniture?" murmured Claude in a dubious tone. "Old furniture? That's soon said! Did we move a step? Did we brush against it? . . . I tell you again that I have gone close up to it twenty times with Mère Chagne or M. Coutelet in the room, and that never . . . Your presence has been sufficient to awaken it; silent to every one else, it stirs to a kind of life for you and me. Doesn't it remind you of an old, deaf, blind, lame dog, who, for all that, feels the approach of the master and proclaims it?"

"What an imagination!" sneered M. de Marbois. "I can understand that your mind is getting unbalanced among all this old rubbish . . ."

"My mind unbalanced?" cried Claude, putting the globe on the lamp which he had just lighted. "You mean that for the first time in my life, my mind has recovered its balance. Devil take Paris, and its enervating life! Here all is discretion and repose. See how orderly everything around us is . . ."

Since the evening before he had put the room tidy, and now invited admiration of its beautiful neatness:

"Is not everything just as it used to be? I have left it as it was the day I arrived. The furniture is in the same place, the knick-knacks have not been moved an inch, and . . . forgive me this rather ridiculous care . . . I have even respected the dust, here and there where there appeared to be a finger-mark or the light brush of a sleeve. In other words, if, as I believe, spirits revisit the places they inhabited, those who haunt this house may wander all over it as they please. I have sat up very late once or twice in this room; each time I had the feeling that I was not alone.

But I am keeping you up; you must be tired out with your journey, agitated by this return to the scenes of your youth, and I would not, for the world, keep you any longer from going to bed. This is your bedroom; I have done my best to think of everything you may want . . . If by chance I have forgotten anything do not mind telling me . . . Is one pillow sufficient? Will one lamp give light enough? Here is a glass of water and some matches. I have put a book on the table beside you in case you are not able to sleep. If it is not to your liking, forgive me, I made the choice as I should have done for myself. It is a book I found on one of the shelves, and that I have read over and over again."

"You think of everything," remarked M. de Marbois, turning over the pages of *Clair de Lune* and putting it back on the table.

"I do my best to," answered Claude. "All that I have to add is that you are at home here, that the keys are in the drawers so that if the fancy takes you, you can open them. Sleep well, do not be afraid of the ghosts. I say that, because the country-folk here are superstitious, and made the same remark to me when I first came to Trois-Tourelles. But I have learned not to fear Those-who-return; I even confess to a certain liking for them, and, believe, without flattering myself too much, that they return the compliment. And now, good-night, sleep well."

XII

CLAUDE went towards his room, opened the door with a clatter, shut it again, but did not go in, and went noiselessly down the stairs into the garden.

Out there it was adorably silent. The lawns glimmered like velvet in the moonlight; the flowers that still bloomed sent out perfumes that thrilled one all the more, because neither their shape nor their color could be discerned in the darkness; slugs had left shining tracks on the grass; a huge toad was going the round of the flower-beds. The lighted window of M. de Marbois' room alone broke the harmonious nocturne. Claude seated himself on a bench so that he might gaze at it.

Now and then a shadow passed before the curtains. Once it stopped, the window opened, the light, no longer shaded by the lace curtains, appeared, dazzling, and M. de Marbois leaned out.

Presently, however, he drew back, closed the shutters, pulled the curtains together, and nothing remained of the light but a faint glimmer, until that too vanished at last, and the darkness and silence were complete.

With his eyes fixed on the window, heedless of the cool night air that stirred the branches, Claude sat whistling under his breath. The moon and the stars pursued their journey above him, and, following their imperceptible movement, he ecstatically imagined himself the master of the universe.

An hour went by thus, and then another. He began to show signs of impatience, leaning to the right, then to the left, stretching out his neck, listening intently. Three o'clock struck. Almost at the same moment a flash of light gleamed from M. de Marbois' window. At once Claude sat still, a strange smile on his face.

Anyone looking at him would have thought he could see what was taking place behind those walls. Presently he got up from the bench, crossed the lawn, entered the house, went upstairs on tiptoe, down the corridor, and arrived at the library door, which he opened.

M. de Marbois, half-dressed, stood with his back to him.

"Who is there?" he cried as he heard the noise.

"It's only I, don't be frightened," said Claude.

"What do you want?"

"I'm rather like the owls," explained Claude. "I can only see and hear clearly at night. Thinking I heard you call, like a host mindful of his guest's comfort, I hastened to your help. That's all."

M. de Marbois drew a hand across his brow and sighed.

"That's all . . . or nearly," Claude corrected himself as he urged him slowly towards the bedroom.

M. de Marbois was trembling to such an extent, that he had to lean against the bed to keep from falling.

"You seem to be quite overcome," remarked Claude with a smile. "Is it our conversation about Those-who-return, that troubles you so much? Have you seen someone, by chance?"

M. de Marbois attempted a smile.

"What nonsense!"

"I must admit," went on Claude, "that just at this moment I cannot see any, but maybe they are hiding? . . . Let us look for them together, shall we? I feel sure that you will not be afraid to look now that I am with you, and my eyes are so sharp they will be able to discover their hiding-place, when they try to slip out of sight."

He lifted the curtains, shook them, opened the dressing-room door, came back to the middle of the room, and pulled aside a hanging.

"Stop that foolery!" said M. de Marbois indistinctly.

"Foolery?" cried Claude. "How irreverently you speak! At such a time and in such a place it would be more seemly to measure your words . . . But I see that your fear is feigned, and that you are making fun of me . . . Or is it a bad dream from which you have not yet recovered, that disturbed your sleep? . . . I may have put some fantastic story on your table . . . This one is open, you have read it, and imagination encroaching on reality . . . Of course; it is *Apparition*. That story has given me some ghastly hours too. It is not a nice book to read at night, I might even say that it made you open the writing desk?"

"Of course not . . ." said M. de Marbois.

"Be careful," answered Claude, "or you will make me think that someone, neither you nor I, has come into this room. I observe the smallest details with great care. A little while ago, the key was vertical in the lock, and now it is horizontal."

"I must have touched it without meaning to."

"That's possible . . . Everything is possible . . . But there is a very easy way to find out . . ."

He let down the flap, suddenly turned completely around, and cried out.

"Devil take it! The Spirits have gotten a finger in the pie, or a thief has gotten into the room! There was a telegram in that pigeon-hole just before you came in here . . ."

"A telegram?" murmured M. de Marbois in a voice that was almost inaudible.

"Yes, a telegram, an old, a very old telegram . . . It's been stolen."

"What's the use of worrying? was the telegram so important?"

"So important that I would give one of my arms to have it back! Ah! but it's got to be found!"

He went to the window, calling:

"Madame Chagne!"

"Are you mad? You would wake the house for a scrap of paper? Very well, then, yes . . . I took that telegram . . . I burned it . . . not thinking what I was doing . . . What about it?"

Claude planted himself before him with folded arms:

"And it never occurred to you that the fact of its having been kept for thirty years showed it to be of great value? But wait a moment . . . there was something else! Some newspapers; did you burn them too, 'Not thinking?'"

He rushed to the fireplace, and, finding it empty, burst into a fit of laughter:

"I told you there were ghosts! Ah! an old and terrible story is coming to an end!"

"Claude, my child!"

M. de Marbois staggered. Claude seized him firmly by the arm, and dragged him to the library:

"You did not expect this? Thirty years have passed since that night of August 12th, 1880, and the story is as fresh as the dawn of the day that followed it! Would you like me to tell it to you as it was told me by the things that surround me? Now, dare you tell me there are no Spirits! Of course, they only show themselves when they feel inclined, and when a little encouragement is forthcoming. It looks as though they were disposed to be friendly towards me, as they have led me to the truth . . . But first of all give me back that telegram and the papers that you did not burn."

M. de Marbois pulled a bundle of papers crumpled from his pocket, and held them out, stammering:

"Claude, my child . . . !"

"There is no doubt," went on Claude, "that you are not the strong-minded man I thought you . . . Had I been in your place, I would have died rather than give them back . . . Now you dare not look me straight in the face. You can tell that I know . . . and I know more than you dare think."

He laughed, comfortably seated in the armchair. After giving vent to his delight, he got up, and, in a serious voice, began:

"It is not for me to judge my mother; whatever sins she may have committed were most surely remitted by what she suffered through you. Anyone can forgive a poor girl who turns aside from the right path to escape destitution. M. DeGuy looked on things in that light, seeing that after providing for her for the time being, it was his intention to assure her future by marrying her."

M. de Marbois was trembling; Claude took no notice of him:

"But let us go on, let us go on . . . When she was only a poor girl you would not marry her, and you were careful not to seduce her. Once her lot was cast in with another's, things took on a different aspect. You appear on the scenes again . . . you return to the assault . . . You come to the house, to their house at night. M. DeGuy comes suddenly upon you here, in this very room. He is old, you are young . . . You might get away, but you think that after such an escapade, the will in favor of the wretched woman will be annulled, the fortune escape you . . . and you remain. Ah! it doesn't take long, or rather it does take long, horribly long. A blow, strangling, would leave traces . . . you are no such fool! . . . You seize him in your arms, and press, until the breath leaves his body, until he suffocates, until he falls. You wait until life is extinct . . . Then, and then alone, you let him go!"

M. de Marbois shook his head feebly. Claude burst into a terrible laugh:

"What do you think about it? A little imagination has been sufficient to reconstruct the drama, has it not?"

M. de Marbois stammered:

"You dare . . . to your father . . ."

Claude's face became terrible in its gravity:

"You my father? Look here!"

He stretched out his wide-open hands. M de Marbois tried to utter a cry, but not a sound came from his mouth, and, putting up a hand to hide his face, he fell backwards.

"Now," said Claude, "it's your turn, my boy!"

He was standing with one foot on each side of the body, and muttered as he turned up his sleeves:

"This time I know why I am going to kill. This time it is not a poor dog whose torture I look on at, without knowing why, or a little girl that I am compelled to strangle when I thought I wanted to kiss her mouth . . ."

He put his fingers round the neck:

"You are shamming dead; you think I shall not have the strength nor the courage? I have both. I would rather you made a fight for it though, that you tried to scream, or bite, or struggle; and to prove it . . ."

M. de Marbois did not stir; his eyes turned up and showing the whites, seemed sightless; his face was bloodless.

Claude relaxed his grip and put a hand on the heart:

"Look here, you're not going to fool me by dying of fright I hope? . . . No you're breathing, God be praised!"

He was about to continue his task, when suddenly he stood upright and sneered:

"Death is nothing. The only thing that's worth while is to watch its approach! . . . Who would not choose to die like this, unconscious of everything? . . . You deserve a better fate, my good man!"

And he went out on tip-toe.

XIII

MÈRE CHAGNE was feeding the chickens. Each time she threw a handful of grain into the air, she called, "Coopy! Coopy! Coopy!" She did this rhythmically and steadily, like a person who had done the same thing thousands of times, and, as the creatures pecked at her feet, she looked at the sky, and at the early autumn trees, to whose gold-tipped foliage a reflection of the summer sun still seemed to cling.

Although it was nearly eleven o'clock in the morning, the shutters of the master's house were still closed. Now and then, without slackening or hastening her work, she glanced at them.

"Good-morning, Mère Chagne!" cried Claude.

In her surprise she nearly let the corner of her apron go, and spilled the grain.

For two weeks, Claude had kept so much to himself, greeting people with such surly looks and speech, that his calm and cheerful voice amazed her:

"Fine day, isn't it?"

She could hardly believe her eyes; was that M. Claude who only yesterday was shut in his room, with an old shawl wrapped round his shoulders, his hair tousled, his face unshaven, so bent and pale-faced, that when you caught a glimpse of him with his eyes glued to the window he looked like a ghost? . . .

This morning, clad in a Norfolk coat, and brown gaiters, with his face clean-shaven, and hair carefully arranged, he looked like another man.

Dipping a hand into the old woman's apron, Claude scattered the grain, calling to the chickens as she did. But they hesitated. He began to laugh.

"Just look at that! I give them food, and they only take to their heels."

"Dumb creatures are like people," explained Mère Chagne, "they only know who looks after them. If the master would only come here a few times, they would not be frightened, and would eat out of your hand."

"Well, I'll come," he assured her, "it will amuse me. They're fine birds; what would they fetch at market?"

"Fed as these are? Not less than twenty francs a pair . . . when you come to think of what it costs to feed them."

She spoke garrulously, glad to find her master interested in her work. He listened, questioning her as he had done when he first came to the place, in the days when he had not yet crossed the threshold of the library, and was learning the ABCs of his new life.

Chagne came up. Claude inquired about the sheep and the oxen, the price of the hay, and the produce of the vegetable garden. He asked to see what vegetables had been planted, the dairy which smelt of sour milk, and the hutches where the rabbits were nibbling cabbage leaves with quick and anxious veracity. Up at the farm, Chagne showed him a hare he had killed himself that morning.

"I spotted him so near the house, that after I had fired I wished I hadn't, for fear it should wake the master."

"I heard nothing," said Claude.

"The master sleeps well, he is young."

Claude was feeling where the shot had struck the creature. Mère Chagne held out her apron for him to wipe his hands. He praised Père Chagne for his smart shooting, and said he was sorry he had not been up to see it. Chagne told him he knew the whereabouts of another and bigger hare, and that if he liked they would try to get him.

"That's a good idea," said Claude approvingly.

As they chatted, they came around to the house again. From the lane came the sound of running footsteps and laughter.

"It's the children coming out of school," said Mère Chagne in explanation.

"What time is it then?"

"Eleven o'clock."

"And my father still asleep!"

"Monsieur was tired after the journey," said the farmer.

"Tired?" said Claude, in the jesting voice of a man who does not know what it is to be lazy and lie abed. "One is never tired in the country!"

"Oh!" ventured Mère Chagne, winking her eye, "the master is feeling very strong and well this morning; he hasn't always felt that way!"

Claude agreed:

"I was wrong; today the fresh air alone has made me feel better. All the more reason that I should wake up my father. Take his breakfast up to him and tell him how delightful it is here under the trees."

Mère Chagne went into the kitchen. He watched her while she arranged a tray with hot coffee, warm milk, slices of brown bread and a pot of butter. Père Chagne who had plenty to say as soon as shooting was in question, told Claude of a place where he would find as many rabbits as he wanted, and a field, where, as soon as the sun burst through the morning mists, larks were as plentiful as flies round a bit of sugar.

"We don't touch them, seeing as how shot is dear, but it will amuse the master who doesn't mind about that."

A scream made them start, and at the same moment they turned round. At a window on the first floor, between the shutters that flapped backwards and forewards, arms uplifted, Mère Chagne appeared.

"What is the matter?" cried Claude.

"The master's father, Monsieur! the master's father!"

Breathless with excitement, she could not say another word. Claude rushed to the house, followed by Chagne, ran up the stairs three at a time, and stopped at the door of the library.

As the old Chagnes were about to kneel down, and lift up M. de Marbois, he thrust them aside. Mère Chagne was biting the corner of her apron.

"Mother of mercy! is he dead?"

Claude dared not touch the body; Père Chagne murmured:

"He's breathing."

She crossed herself thankfully, and as Claude slipped his hand under his father's head, she stammered:

"He cut his head falling! . . . the master's hands are covered with blood!"

"Nothing of the kind," said Claude, glancing at them, "they're that color, as you very well know."

She crossed herself a second time, then, reassured, speech became imperative:

"It's as if . . ."

Père Chagne nudged her with his elbow; she stopped. Claude looked fixedly at her for a moment, she colored and went on:

"It's as if M. de Comte had seen something that frightened him . . . Look, he has hidden his face with his arm . . ."

"That's true," Claude admitted.

Then he took hold of the body under his arms.

"You take his legs," he ordered.

Père Chagne slowly bent down.

"Let us carry him to my bed," said Claude.

And as the old man hesitated, he added:

"What are you waiting for?"

"Perhaps it would be better to leave M. le Comte as he is, until the arrival of . . ."

"Of whom?"

". . . Of no one master," replied the farmer, lifting the legs.

As soon as he was laid upon the bed, M. de Marbois opened his eyes.

"Well, father?" said Claude, bending over him. "What has happened to you?"

M. de Marbois' lips moved, but nothing came from them but a meaningless sound.

"Lie still," said Claude. "M. Chagne, go and let M. Coutelet know. Get a hot-water bottle ready, Mme. Chagne, then you can light the fire."

M. de Marbois still held his arm over his face; after a moment he asked for something to drink. Claude poured some water in a glass, added a few drops of peppermint cordial and held it to him. While he went away from the bedside, M. de Marbois put his arm down and opened his eyes. When he saw Claude, he smiled. Then, suddenly the smile became fixed, and his cheeks livid. When Claude brought the glass nearer his lips he turned his head, and tried to push away the hand stretched out to him. It was Claude's turn to smile:

"Come, let me look after you."

He gently held down the arm with his left hand. As the glass touched his teeth, M. de Marbois threw his head back, and a few drops of the liquid spattered his face; one fell on his lips, he wiped it off with the back of his fingers:

"Come," insisted Claude, "be reasonable."

With his face hidden in his arm again, M. de Marbois refused:

"No . . . no . . . I saw . . ."

"What did you see?"

"I saw you . . . pour . . ."

"This?" said Claude, holding up a bottle. "It's a cordial. Drink . . ."

"Must I?" said M. de Marbois more audibly.

"I advise you to."

M. de Marbois took the glass between his two hands, held it up for a moment, and swallowed a mouthful. After which he gave it back and lay down again on his pillow. But his eyes were not so tightly shut that he did not see Claude drink what was left in the glass, and take up his motionless guard at the foot of the bed again. This reassured him, and at the same time, the cool drink revived him; he breathed more freely, his color came back, and he murmured:

"I beg forgiveness . . ."

Claude did not stir. He repeated: "I beg forgiveness," so

distinctly this time, that Claude said:

"Of whom do you beg forgiveness, and for what?"

"Of the man I . . ."

He stopped; Claude waited for him to finish his sentence. But the words he now had to pronounce were doubtless so terrible, that his courage failed him, and he contented himself with saying in a hollow voice:

"You know . . ."

"I know nothing, but I think you need rest; try to sleep."

"I have dreamt of a judge, sometimes, but I never imagined one so dreadful as you," said M. de Marbois.

"Go to sleep!" repeated Claude.

Down in the kitchen, while she broke pieces of wood across her knee, Mère Chagne said to her husband:

"Isn't it strange? . . . In the very same place as M. De Guy, as though it had been done on purpose! . . ."

Without replying, Père Chagne whistled to his dog, and went out.

XIV

WHEN he arrived M. Coutelet found Claude sitting beside his father's bed. He had feared a greater misfortune, and cried out in his relief:

"So have you given us a good fright now, M. de Marbois? What happened?"

He addressed the question to both. Claude answered:

"I don't know at all. Last night, when I left you, I went in to say goodnight to my father; he seemed perfectly well. As the night was warm, I went for a stroll in the garden, and then I went to bed. I got up early, and was having a look around the place, when, at about eleven o'clock, Mère Chagne, who had taken up his breakfast, found him lying on the library floor. I sent for you at once; that is all I know."

M. Coutelet took hold of M. de Marbois' wrist:

"The pulse is steady . . . a little quick but not feverish."

He felt his temples and ankles, and rubbed a thumbnail on his forehead:

"Your arteries are like a young man's; you will soon be all right."

M. de Marbois smiled faintly; the apothecary went on:

"Have you any pain? . . . you have? . . . you feel bruised all over, and your head aches, doesn't it? I don't wonder!

It came into contact with the floor, you must have fallen straight backwards."

"I don't remember," answered M. de Marbois.

"You had no feeling of discomfort before it happened?"

"Perhaps . . ."

"Palpitations?"

"Maybe . . . I cannot remember . . ."

"You didn't reach up to get a book down from one of the shelves?"

"I'm very tired," murmured M. de Marbois.

"We are going to leave you in peace; we will discuss the whole thing again, when you have slept a few hours."

He patted his hand encouragingly and went out. Claude went with him. As they passed in front of the bookcase, M. Coutelet pointed to a place where the carpet was turned up:

"Was it here he fell?"

"It was here he was found."

"Indeed," remarked M. Coutelet, "and you haven't the least notion what can have taken place? A man as strong as he is does not fall down in a faint for no reason . . . Have you never known him to be ill?"

"Never."

"At present I think there is no danger, but later he must be examined by a doctor. He must be supervised . . . It's a pity I didn't see what position he was lying in when he was found. Sometimes a mere attitude helps the diagnosis. Thus, for example, a man will come to you, holding his arm in a certain position, which tells its own tale; fracture of the arm. Another bends over, with his hand pressed flat over his thorax: a fractured rib . . ."

He went on, giving example after example, less for the sake of showing his knowledge, than for the pleasure of talking of what he had learned by experience, and proved by books. He also did it to hide his uneasiness and preoccupation. Claude's mood a few days before his father's arrival, the sudden disappearance of his mad ideas, his attitude the night before, now moody, now jovial, a thousand things he had said at different times, the strange coincidence of M. de Marbois' collapse on the very spot where M. DeGuy had been found, all these things worried him, and excited his curiosity.

There was something between the account given of the affair, and the truth, that was very certain . . . but what was it? He stopped what he was saying, and asked point-blank:

"What about you? Were you all right last night?"

His doubt was becoming more definite. He remembered the incident of little Marie, and the excited state in which he had found Claude the following day. Supposing that a similar had occurred, it was only natural that M. de Marbois should be anxious not to reveal the fact. That must be the reason for his reticent, and vague replies . . .

He considered that his own responsibility was seriously involved in the matter. He alone knew of Claude's morbid condition, and the dangerous lengths to which such a maniac might go. Had he taken things too lightly when he had not told the father exactly how they stood, and when he called "neurasthenia" what might, perhaps, be more serious?

He made up his mind to have a confidential talk with M. de Marbois as soon as possible; speaking as man to man, he would end by knowing the truth.

Claude did not seem to be aware of the mental travail going on within him, and answered:

"I? I never slept better in my life."

He spoke so calmly that M. Coutelet doubted his own logic. Besides, Claude had gone back to the first part of their conversation.

"You were saying that a person's attitude may help one to diagnose; that is when it relates to a surgical case, I imagine, but what about a medical case? . . ."

"A medical case," cried the apothecary, carried away by his subject, "why, my dear fellow, the most extraordinary things have been known to happen. I can remember . . . many years ago when I was completing my studies in Paris . . . a man who was found dead in bed. His servant was suspected of having killed him, in order to rob him, and, *ma foi*, they were actually on the point of arresting him, when somebody was so struck with the expression of horror still reflected in the dead man's eyes, that he was impelled to follow the direction of the look, the trajectory, so to speak, and saw, at the culminating point, a monstrous, and horrible spider. When he had caught sight of it, the old man had died of fright; syncope, sudden stopping of the heart, that sort of thing is well-known."

"What you tell me is strange," said Claude thoughtfully. "Now I remember a detail to which I attached no importance, and to which Mère Chagne called my attention. M de Marbois, my father, had his head hidden under his arm when we found him, so firmly too, that when I put him on the bed I had to make two attempts to bring his arm back to its normal position."

"Ah!" exclaimed M. Coutelet, triumphantly, "here is something definite. We must follow that clue. Come with me."

They turned on their steps, and went back to the library. M. Coutelet placed himself opposite the bookcase, standing in the same position that M. de Marbois must have done, when he fell, and looked straight ahead, to the right, to the left, and seeing nothing out of the ordinary, shook his head. But as he looked down at his feet, he saw the book that had not been picked up, and said:

"Your father has the same taste as you, he was reading *Apparition!*"

"Can it be that which impressed him to such an extent?" murmured Claude.

"You surely don't think that," answered M. Coutelet with a smile.

"I'm not thinking, I'm asking?" Claude corrected him.

"No," M. Coutelet assured him, "we must look elsewhere."

"Then we will look," answered Claude. "But excuse me if I don't go to the gate with you; my father might be wanting me."

XV

MÈRE CHAGNE kept Claude company by his father's bedside for several hours. When night came on, she left them. Suddenly, M de Marbois, who until then had appeared to be sleeping, tried to get up. Claude stopped him.

"Are you not comfortable here? Where would you be better? You yourself assured me this was my mother's favorite room; it must be full of memories for you . . ."

"I wish to get up," said M. de Marbois decidedly. "I wish to leave this house. You will never hear of me again . . . I will leave you all I possess."

"Why speak of departure, of exile and of giving me all your fortune? On the contrary, you will remain here."

"Yes, yes," murmured M. de Marbois, "you want a public confession . . . Yesterday, when I arrived, I felt that you knew . . . That portrait, the book on my table . . . the telegram . . . this room where you have forced me to sleep . . ."

"A portrait? A book? A telegram? . . . There is only mother's portrait here; I could not possibly tell you what book I put on your table, and as for the telegram, I have not received one since I came to Trois-Tourelles . . ."

"Your silent entry . . . your challenge . . ." went on M. de Marbois.

Claude appeared lost in amazement.

"I came in? I spoke to you? How could I have? After taking you to your room, I went out with M. Coutelet, and did not see you again."

"You did not come back here?"

"No."

"You did not show me a photograph?"

"Certainly not."

"You did not tell me someone had forced open the writing-desk?"

"I said to you: 'Father, this your room; sleep well, and if you want anything call me.' I said nothing else."

"What is the good of lying, and speaking so kindly to me?" murmured M. de Marbois.

"Why should I lie, and why should I speak to you other than I do? By the way, you mentioned the writing-desk. Would you let me have the key of it?"

"It's in the lock," said M. de Marbois in a voice that was hardly audible.

Claude went to the next room, opened the desk, and took out a piece of paper:

"Do you mean this?"

M. de Marbois uttered a cry:

"Give it to me."

"Here it is."

He read the telegram and was about to crumple it in his fingers. Claude took it from him in the most natural way and replaced it where he had found it, then, as he heard M. Coutelet talking to Mère Chagne in the garden, he went to meet him.

"How's the patient?" asked the old man.

"Not very well. After a few hours' sleep he woke in a state of great excitement. He tries to get up, utters words that seem senseless to me, cries that he is caught in a trap . . ."

"The devil!" ejaculated M. Coutelet, "that looks like the mania of persecution."

"Is that serious?"

M. Coutelet pursed up his lips without replying.

They had reached the door. Seated on his bed, his knees drawn up under his chin, M. de Marbois' face was hidden in his hands. At the sound of their footsteps, he jerked upright; M. Coutelet was struck by the violent start, but, without showing it, began a friendly conversation with him, in which he provided both questions and answers. M. de Marbois seemed oblivious of everything. His eyes, now fixed in a glare, now roving round, refused to meet another's. Once, wishing to force him to look him in the face, M. Coutelet caught hold of his shoulder. But he threw himself back with a scream, and, as the apothecary attempted to continue the conversation, he replied in a plaintive voice:

"I remember nothing . . . between the time when I undressed, and when I woke up in my bed, there is a gap . . . a great gap . . ."

"Yet," put in Claude, "were you not telling me just now that someone had followed you into this room?"

"I can't remember . . ."

"You also said something about a book . . ."

"Do what you like," stammered M. de Marbois, closing his eyes, "I am waiting . . ."

"What are you waiting for?" asked M. Coutelet, curious to find what the irrelevant reply meant.

M. de Marbois jerked his head towards Claude:
"He knows..."

M. Coutelet thought all persistence useless, said a few more encouraging words, and signed to Claude to follow him into the library:

"What is your opinion?" asked Claude as soon as they were alone.

"Not very encouraging," grunted the apothecary, in the tone of a man worried by thoughts he would prefer not to express. He rubbed his chin, tapped his finger-tips on the books that lay upon the table.

"You are not anxious in any way?" asked Claude. His quiet manner induced Coutelet to reply:

"Yes, my boy, I am, and seriously too... I am no savant, my science does not go much higher than that of a quack, but a quack sees things in the true light very often, because, when making a diagnosis, he often does not bother about the exceptions that worry the doctors... You can, therefore, accept my opinion, with reservations... although... Anyhow, were I in your place, I should send for a specialist from Paris... This morning it looked like a delirium brought on by a bad dream, or by hallucination when in a waking state... Now I fear the cause of the trouble is more deeply seated. A bad dream does not last four and twenty hours, daylight disposes of the fancies bred of night, and it is the same with hallucination..."

"But then," murmured Claude, "do you mean that my father is..."

The door opened violently. M. de Marbois appeared:

"What are you waiting for? Do I look like a man who is trying to escape? I am ready, take me away. But no more pretense, no more plotting. Let us have done with it, I am here!"

He stretched out his arms and crossed his wrists. Claude was about to reply, but M. Coutelet forestalled him:

"Of course."

M. de Marbois went back into his room; Claude looked at the apothecary:

"Why did you say that?"

"Because you must never contradict patients like that. You must not argue with a man who has a fixed idea in his head. The words your father said are evidently the result of such a thought . . . if you can call such a disconcerting and fantastic jumble by such a name . . . But do we know what that thought is? . . . And if we knew it, what good would it be to reason, where reason no longer is."

"Oh!" ejaculated Claude with a start.

This time the word had been said. After having turned it round and round in his mouth, and kept it back on his lips, old Coutelet felt relieved at having let it out, and began a long speech.

In the mediocrity of his present existence, the honest fellow had never forgotten the ambitions of his youth. At the back of his little shop, where all his knowledge resolved itself into the compounding of ointments and pills, commonplace duties, almost the same as those of a very fussy grocer, he loved to embellish his conversation with the souvenirs of his student days. A passion to show off his learning was rather a weak spot with him. Thus, forgetting that he was speaking of a father to his son he began a veritable lecture:

"What is madness? A lesion, more or less serious, of the intellectual and mental faculties? The causes of it? So diverse in their kinds that I will not try to explain them to you.

"Here we have before us one who believes himself to be the victim of persecution; his conversation, his gestures, his attitude, everything points to it. The crisis now taking place is nothing but the climax of a thousand small crises that have already taken place without our knowledge.

"Furious as he was a few moments since, he is perhaps calm at this very moment. A deceiving calm that the smallest excitement would break. For these sufferers, forgetfulness is only momentary. That is why I advise you not to allude to anything that has taken place when you return to him . . . Now I tell you once again, the only person who can decide the matter is a specialist. Believe me, it would be wise to send for one at once . . . What about Dr. Charlier, for instance? . . . I mention him . . . but if you have anyone else to suggest . . ."

"Not in the least . . . If you really consider it necessary to send for him . . ."

"Indispensably so . . ."

"Then will you be good enough to send for him?"

"He can get here within forty-eight hours."

"And," said Claude slowly, "what do you think he will order?"

"Confinement in an asylum without the slightest doubt."

"How awful!" murmured Claude, hiding his face in his hands.

But behind them, he began to laugh so hard, that he had to bite his lips in order to stop.

XVI

INSTEAD of returning to M. de Marbois' room, Claude went round, crossed a passage, and looked through a keyhole. Standing before the window, M. de Marbois was looking out into the garden, without daring, however, to go close up where he could be seen in the broad daylight. Now and then a shudder convulsed him, and he made as though to hide his face behind his arm again in the same way that had struck Mère Chagne so much. Then he drew a hand across the back of his neck, and a hoarse cry escaped him. Suddenly he began to run round and round the room, hitting at the wall with his fists.

Claude sneered:

"Growl away, bang away, the four walls are strong!"

This state of panic, which resembled that of a trapped beast, was followed by exhaustion, and flinging himself into an armchair M. de Marbois began to mutter unintelligible words.

"Oh!" thought Claude, "things are moving too rapidly, much too rapidly!"

His hate was counting on a more long-drawn-out feast. If he had overcome his desire to kill the evening before, it was in order to gloat over his victory, to taste its delights, to keep it going as he liked with his alternate kind words and threats.

A moment ago when M. Coutelet had mentioned the word asylum, he had laughed in his sleeve, because he knew, that in spite of appearances, M. de Marbois was not mad, and that uncertainty as to whether he was trying to spare him or ruin him was the only reason for his incoherent replies, his fits of rage, and half-avowals which none but he himself could understand.

Now he began to wonder whether the old man was right, whether he was assisting at the shipwreck of that unyielding sanity the serenity of which had never been disturbed by any threat. If that were the case, goodbye to punishment. In a few hours M. de Marbois would be nothing but a rag of humanity; you could insult, ill-treat, and take him away, without his realizing anything.

Truly, if his vengeance were to end at that, what a sell! It would be better to strike while a glimmer of reason remained. At least he would taste the physical joy of killing; that it would only last for a moment, he knew; but what a moment, and what a joy!

While he was thinking these things, M. de Marbois turned round and he saw his face in the full light of day.

These hours of waiting had turned him from the strong, handsome man that he was only yesterday, into an old one. His body was bent, his hands hung limp; under the open shirt collar his neck looked stringy; his cheek-bones stood out, his cheeks had fallen in, and his dim eyes looked upwards like the eyes of a condemned man on his way to the scaffold.

The sight was sweet to Claude! Truly he had accomplished a great work! He, the weak creature, whose opinion, whose requests, even whose presence was despised; he who had gone through life as though apologizing for being there at all; he who was filled with wonder at the least bold move, he had done this thing!

He would have liked people to be able to see him confront this man and to say to them: "Which of us is afraid now, he or I?"

And yet he had not the courage to push open the door. Broken as he was, M. de Marbois still dominated him. No one can tremble during twenty years at the mere sight of a person, without something of that fear remaining behind; it is long before the dog turned wolf again does not start at the sound of the whip, and oppressed peoples, even in apparent revolt, keep, for generations, the frightened timidity of slaves.

M. de Marbois leaped to his feet, ran to the window, and opened it. Claude thought he was going to throw himself out and have done with it . . . Fear of this dispersed all other fears, and he rushed into the room. Surprised at the suddenness of his appearance, M. de Marbois stopped.

"Ouf!" sighed Claude, "you did give me a fright!"

The words were simple, even affectionate, and in no way differed from those he had spoken since the day before. But his tone was so pointed that M. de Marbois felt his flesh go icy cold. Besides, Claude had given up pretending. After looking at his father from head to foot with the cynical air of a horse-dealer, he sat astride the arm of a chair and remarked:

"Well, and how goes it?"

M. de Marbois looked hard at the door.

"Ah, yes," said Claude, as he went to close it, "you are expecting a visitor, I believe? But he will not be here for awhile . . . Just a little later . . ."

M. de Marbois did not move; Claude pointed to a chair opposite his:

"We are in no hurry; we have so much to say to one another.

"Now confess that you were surprised at my kindness this morning. You said to yourself: 'that fellow is going off his head! After trying to kill me, here he is, surrounding me with the tenderest care; after accusing me of a crime he makes not the least allusion to it.' This sort of thing is enough to unhinge the most well-balanced brain. The whole thing is so bewildering, I wouldn't mind betting that you have gone so far as to ask yourself if *you* are not the one to be going out of your mind; and if the scene that took place was not a bad dream? . . . That's it, isn't it? I have guessed; you are hesitating between the real and the unreal; at this very moment you cannot make up your mind . . . It must be a very unpleasant sensation not to be sure of one's sanity . . . You say no word but your hands are eloquent. Come! A little more nerve! Devil take it, control yourself! You are going to need all your courage, for what you have seen and heard is nothing to what remains for you to see and hear.

"And first of all let me explain.

"If I spared you last night, it was not because of any fine feeling. Pity is unknown to me; from whom should I have learned it? . . . I had made up my mind to make you go mad, and 'pon my soul you were on the right track. I bet that at this moment you would not dare assert that I came into your room last night, nor to deny it . . . My wish was that you should lose your reason slowly with here and there a lucid interval, that you should feel madness prowling around you, full of temptations and threats, something in the nature of what I have endured for such long years . . . only more so.

"But you really are not the strong-minded person I thought you! You staggered at the first onslaught . . . it's hardly conceivable to one who knew you for such a devil of a fellow! But there! you would have been raving mad in less than forty-eight hours on the treatment I had prescribed for you! A little while ago, I was watching you through this keyhole; you were pitiable. You didn't think that anyone could see you, did you? Now that is exactly what is worrying me, for it points to a terrific mental collapse in you. Suppose that somebody, a detective, for instance, had been watching you instead of me . . . it would have settled his conviction, and you would have been done for . . . In the same way, so I've been told, examining magistrates have a certain number of tests, more or less infallible, calculated to make their prisoners confess; cross-examination at night, for instance, by the dim light of one lamp. Darkness . . . Silence . . . what auxillaries! . . . There is also physical fatigue. They forget to supply the accused with a chair, they keep him standing for one hour, two hours, and when, exhausted, he asks to sit down, they take no notice and go on with the inquiry . . .

"I would have made a good examining magistrate. But with a criminal like you there wouldn't have been much pleasure in it; it is too easy. Think what you confessed when that good man, M. Coutelet, was here!"

For the first time M. de Marbois opened his lips:

"I?"

"Yes, indeed, in so many words. Only it never entered the head of that most excellent man that you were a murderer, and he put it down to mania; a particular kind of mania, lasting and dangerous . . . He even gave it a name; *the mania of persecution*. And, as you know, when a doctor

. . . and he is that to all extents and purposes . . . gives a name to an illness, the patient is bound to consent to have it."

This jest seemed to him such a merry one, that he burst into laughter, slapping his knees:

"Whatever fault I may have committed," began M. de Marbois.

"Fault? Gad, you are modest!"

"Whatever crime," the wretched man corrected himself.

"That's better," exclaimed Claude.

"Remember that your mother . . ."

As the words left his mouth Claude rushed at him with uplifted hand:

"Don't bring her name into all this! I can guess what you are coward enough to suggest, but I will not allow it! Not much! You would like to make me believe that she was your accomplice . . ."

"That is not what I was about to say," murmured M. de Marbois. "Remember that your mother bore my name . . . that it is yours, too . . ."

"Ah!" exclaimed Claude with a sigh of relief, "that is good to hear! You are not as mad as I thought, indeed you are not mad at all, since in the middle of such an upheaval you can still find arguments that might convince anyone except myself. Your name? It is not part of me any more than the clothing I wear. It is not my name, I will have none of it. It can be dragged in the gutter without a spatter of dirt touching me. To prove that you are nothing to me, I have only to mention two dates, the date of your marriage, and the date of my birth. No, really, if you have nothing better to offer me . . ."

As he spoke, he got up, and walked slowly up and down the room; M. de Marbois sat with bent head, lost in meditation. But in reality he was on the alert. His muscles, which an instant before had appeared so slack, were gradually becoming taut. By imperceptible jerks he brought his elbows to rest on the arms of the chair again. He leaned against the flat of it, and placed his feet flat on the carpet. Soon his position was adjusted, and as Claude turned his back on him, he raised himself on his hands.

"Hi there!" cried Claude suddenly, facing round on him. "You cannot get rid of me like you did M. Deguy! I am young and suspicious... And what would be the good of that? After you've done away with me as well? A fine advance indeed! I have taken my precautions, my proofs are in a safe place..."

He lied with contemptuous assurance. M. de Marbois realized that he was the weaker and that it was necessary to gain time. However complete Claude's calm might be, he guessed it was but short-lived, and that one of the fits of excitement which he had so often witnessed would suddenly take its place. Then the rôles would be reversed. He would seize him with both hands, Chagne and his wife would come rushing up in answer to his shouts, and it would be proved that the young fellow was mad... If that were not sufficient, if the terrified people hesitated to separate them... well then... he would press... he would press... like the other...

At the thought a faint smile came to his lips. But, already Claude had a new idea and went on:

"Come, we have wasted time enough already! You will realize that I did not come here without knowing what I was about. I have my plan, and will tell it to you. In two days, Dr. Charlier will be my guest. He is a well-known mental specialist, a great celebrity, world famous. Between now and then you must have made up your mind. I might impose my will upon you; I leave you to choose. You see, I am generous . . . When I say choose, I don't mean that exactly. I offer you two solutions. Either you will continue to act madness, and you are such a good actor that the great man will be taken in, or you will confess . . . and that means a cell . . . and I need not tell you what will follow . . .

"Until then I will keep you company. Don't be afraid. I shall not be in your way. If you care for conversation, we will talk. If you prefer silence you shall not hear the sound of my voice. I don't mind one way or the other, and shall be equally delighted to see the handcuffs put on you or the straightjacket. And now allow me to rest, for these two days have rather tried my nerves."

He sat down in an armchair, and stretched out his legs on another.

At mid-day, Mère Chagne brought in lunch, and laid the table for two. Claude deliberately unfolded his napkin, and proferred the dish.

"A little of this excellent fish?"

M. de Marbois pushed the dish away.

"Come, monsieur," said Mère Chagne, "you must eat, it will make you strong; be good."

And as he sat hunching up his shoulders, she persisted in the sing-song baby voice with which you encourage a sulky child:

"It's good, it's very good!"

He thumped the table with his fist:

"Get out you old witch! Get out, the whole lot of you!"

Mère Chagne stood still in blank amazement, holding out a fillet of sole on the end of a fork. Claude winked at her reassuringly and said in a low voice:

"Do not wait, Mère Chagne . . . I will get him to eat when he is quieter."

With his fingers gripping the cloth, grasping his knife with trembling hand, M. de Marbois cast furious glances around him. Claude waited until the worthy soul had closed the door behind her, and remarked:

"You vote for madness then? Very well, it is your concern." He then began to eat again. He had never felt so light-hearted. Calm descended on him. He revelled in its freshness, and in the mentality of a man who has nothing left to desire. The far-off past, veiled in doubt, the horror-laden days preceding the revelation which had devastated his reason, withdrew to make way for perfect peace.

When he had finished his meal, he folded his napkin, rubbed his hands, and with the little shiver down his back which follows on a well-digested meal, he looked out at the garden where rain had brightened up the yellow of the gravel paths, the bronze of the leaves and the green of the grass, and rejoiced at the thought of the coming winter.

Soon the white frost would powder the countryside, the sound of sabots clattering along the hard roads would be heard, the oxen would come along, enveloped in clouds of steam, ice would cover the pond, and, quietly seated by his fireside, he would watch the dance of the flames in the black depth of the hearth.

After he had gazed earnestly at the picture conjured up in his mind, correcting and defining its details, and reveling in the delights of his freedom, the silence began to weigh on him.

Truth to tell, M. de Marbois was most placid for a condemned man; it almost looked as though he realized nothing; and did not understand the suffering contained in the word "cell."

Therefore, in order to fill this gap, he began to talk, in the careless voice he had adopted about an hour ago.

"A madhouse is not really so terrible after all. The companions one meets with there must be anything but dull. Some of them may be dangerous, no doubt, but once the fit is over, they become sociable again. The keepers are a little severe, perhaps. The shower bath? The straightjacket? . . . Bah! when you were proposing to send me away to stay in one of these establishments, you did not trouble . . . I know that if you were classed as 'dangerous' you would enjoy . . . if I may say so . . . a special treatment, for, knowing you as I do, you would prefer isolation in a padded cell to tiresome promiscuity . . ."

"Scoundrel!" growled M. de Marbois, seizing a knife that lay on the table.

Claude burst into a fit of laughter:

"What a pity there is no one to hear you! Shout, threaten, rouse the village, don't let that worry you. Before long Dr. Charlier will be here, and it would be unfortunate if we had made him come here for nothing. But spare yourself the trouble of brandishing that weapon—the real knife is in my pocket. That one has only got a rotten silver blade. Ah, yes! I'm not tired of life yet. Once I could not understand why you cared so much about it; since this morning I do. The parts are reversed, that's all . . . you in prison, and I free. What a juggling of fate! When you go away I'll come and see you there, now and then we will exchange pleasant remarks on either side of the bars, and I will see that you lack nothing. People will say, 'What a good son!'"

He leaned his clenched fists on the table and, bending over with a terrible expression suddenly appearing on his face, added:

"But you and alone know what that means."

M. de Marbois ground his teeth. Claude laughed the louder:

"The cleverest might well be taken in; you are such a good actor. You must behave just like that, and in no other way before Dr. Charlier. At this moment your expression is splendid. I'm not lying . . . look at yourself in that glass; it is not a deceptive glass, it was the first to tell me the beginning of your life story and of mine. Time has not dimmed the clearness of it. Although the years have tarnished it, they could not wipe away the traces of the faces it reflected. Close beside your evil countenance I see that of two souls, my mother and M. Deguy. Take care, they are watching you; there are three of us around you, and those whose spirits alone are present are not the least to be feared."

M. de Marbois lifted a chair and sent it crashing into the mirror. Claude looked at the fragments of glass that lay scattered on the floor, and shook his head:

"The dead are still there, just the same; ask M. Coutelet."

The apothecary had just opened the door; Claude explained matters to him in a pitiful voice.

"He is rather excited, but he's better now, are you not, *father?*"

M. de Marbois threw himself on the bed and hid his face in the pillow.

"Yes," went on Claude, "it happened suddenly, and quite unprovoked. Mère Chagny and I were pressing him to eat, when he began to wave his arms about and to shout."

"Alas!" sighed the apothecary, "I was right. Things are turning out as I expected. Of all the manias, this particular one is the most terrible. When it gets hold of a person, it effaces everything. The patient lives in a constant state of terror ceaselessly obsessed by fears for what he considers his safety. He forgets to eat and drink, so that he may watch the deeds and words of those who surround him; he rushes at his keeper just at the very moment when he appears to have calmed down. I have brought the rope with me, if he becomes dangerous we can pinion him."

"Have you got it with you?"

"Here it is."

Claude opened the parcel, took out the rope, and, with trembling hands, began to feel it. He was filled with such intense joy that he turned away his head to hide the gleam in his eyes. As he helped him, M. Coutelet explained the way to use it:

"First of all you get hold of his feet, and fasten it in a slip knot; then you bring the rope up and put it once around the hips, then up to shoulders, round the arms, and finish off at the wrists. Thus bound, the patient can only wriggle. It's the same principle as the straightjacket."

"Perhaps now that he is quiet it would be a good thing to fix it on," suggested Claude.

"I would rather you waited a little," replied M. Coutelet. "By giving him a good dose of chloral we shall gain a few hours. In the meantime, Dr. Charlier will have arrived."

"Do you think he will?"

"He'll be up at Trois-Tourelles tomorrow evening."

Claude went up to the bed, and leaning over M. de Marbois, said in the same tone as Mère Chagne when she had been urging him to eat:

"Do you hear? Tomorrow the good doctor will be here to look after you."

Leaning closer, he whispered:

"A cell, furnished with strong bars, where you will be able to weep and howl at your ease."

He expected an explosion of rage, which would give him an immediate pretext for pinioning him, but M. de Marbois never stirred. The apothecary laid the rope on the couch, uncorked the bottle of medicine, and gave instructions to leave nothing he could use as a weapon within the patient's reach, and took his departure.

During the night, Claude kept silence. Darkness made him circumspect. Shadows flitted about the room. All around him was a kind of gentle gliding, a murmur of voices seeking one another, and, with his hands stretched out in the empty space, he seemed to take hold of cold gossamer veils. The keenness of his senses was so acute that he saw in the darkness, his ears heard infinitesimal sounds in the silence and, through the walls, the odors of the earth caressed his nostrils.

The sensation was delicious yet terrible. It made him doubt the reality of his existence and ask himself if he were not already in the kingdom of disembodied shapes, a wandering soul among other eager souls, seeking a body into which he could creep for the space of a second. He saluted the phantoms as they passed by; some of them smiled at him, others continued on their way. They were a mute, intangible multitude, the aggregation of millions of vapors, which had once been men. He recognized, but could assign to them neither features nor color. Once he stretched out his arms to a floating form that seemed more ethereal than the others, and cried:

"Is it you, mother?"

And he thought he heard the plaintive voice reply:

"Yes, my child, it is I."

Again he spoke, his eyes filled with tears:

"Oh, mother! What ought I to do?"

The form had already faded away. He thought she had vanished in order to allow him to do the thing he wished. Besides, dawn was breaking, spreading before the window the outline of trees, the masses of clouds, and the wound which the rising sun makes in the side of the somber sky.

Then the notion of reality came to him again, and he went up to the bed on which M. de Marbois lay. M. de Marbois was asleep. His breast rose and fell to his quiet breathing, his hands lay limp, and, judging by his calm face, it was evident that no painful thought troubled his sleep.

This discovery made him pensive. He compared that other's state of mind with his own. He, possessed by the idea of justice alone, was troubled; with retribution at hand, the other man slept.

Soon, the house awoke; the stable doors opened, the dog barked, he heard the cries of the herds, and the voice of Mère Chagne as she scattered bread to her fowls. Then a train passed, whistling, and the church bell tinkled the call to matins.

"Come," said he, tapping M. de Marbois on the shoulder, "you have slept long enough. Make the most of the hours of freedom left to you and look upon the things you will see no more."

The face M. de Marbois turned to him was calm. He threw back the bedclothes, got up, and began to dress. After he had washed himself with much splashing, he brushed his hair, polished his nails on the palm of his hand, took a book, and sat down near the window. Yesterday's pallor had disappeared; his eyes were clear, his gestures tranquil.

Claude began to fidget round him:

"You haven't forgotten that it's this evening?"

M. de Marbois lifted his eyes from his book, shook his head, and became engrossed in his reading again.

After a long silence, broken only by the rustle of the pages, Claude remarked again, as though he were talking to himself:

"I mustn't forget to tell Père Chagne to get the omnibus ready, because they will be taking you away immediately, I imagine."

"What are you talking about?" inquired M. de Marbois without interrupting his reading.

"I'm curious to see how you behave before Dr. Charlier," went on Claude. "That man's eyes will seek out the very depths of your soul."

And as M. de Marbois still kept an obstinate silence, he went on talking about the cell, the shower-bath, the straightjacket, detailing the horrors of perpetual confinement, the shrieks and rages of the lunatics, the anguish of feeling one's reason crumble.

"If the torture seems too great, you can always confess . . . in that way you will escape from this prison, and from life."

M. de Marbois went on reading, and occasionally a smile appeared on his lips. Mère Chagne brought in lunch at twelve o'clock. M. de Marbois put a marker in his book and sat down at table.

"Are you hungry by chance?" sneered Claude, almost suffocating with rage.

"Why should I not be hungry?" answered M. de Marbois.

"I'm glad to see Monsieur is well again," put in Mère Chagne.

"Excellent woman!" remarked M. de Marbois, gratefully pouring himself out a glass of wine. "But you are not eating anything, Claude; you have tired yourself looking after me, my son."

With set teeth and hands gripping the tablecloth, Claude stared at the man who mocked him. In order to hide his agitation, he tried to swallow a piece of bread, but it stuck in his throat. M. de Marbois talked affectionately to him, and ate of everything on the table.

He stopped speaking as soon as Mère Chagne went out, and went on with his reading.

At about four o'clock it began to grow dark. In the most ordinary voice M. de Marbois asked Claude to light the lamp. He replied that he was quite comfortable as he was, and that darkness was conducive to thought.

"As you please," answered M. de Marbois, shutting up his book.

And they sat in silence, side by side, while the sky grew dark. The clock struck seven.

"Come," said Claude, "this is the end. I am obliged to you for having spared me your lamentations, not that they would have moved me to pity, but sensitive and excitable as I know myself to be, I might have used harsh methods in compelling you to keep silence. So we will waste no time over these little formalities. The Paris express arrives at 7:15. I'm going to pinion you, but not too tightly. When the doctor and M. Coutelet come, they will find you ready to start. Let us make haste, the train is whistling: in less than ten minutes they will be here. Your feet first . . . don't you remember M. Coutelet's explanation? . . ."

"Yes, yes," affirmed M. de Marbois.

"Well? . . ."

"Well, I've changed my mind; that is all."

Claude threw down the rope which he was preparing to place in position:

"You prefer to confess?"

"No."

"Then I shall have to accuse you?"

"And what then?"

"What then? . . . the law courts . . . a trip . . . a trip at break of day, or at least, penal servitude . . . a pleasant prospect."

"Not so bad as you say . . . Only it is nothing but a dream. The law is not indulgent, but it knows how to make the best of a bad job. Do the same. Have you never heard of what is called prescription? . . . Even though they proved my guilt a hundred times over . . . and that is not so easy as you seem to think . . . I have nothing to fear from the law. Had I invented that law myself, I could not have done it better . . . That I shall have to render up my account someday, elsewhere, is a matter that concerns the devil and myself. In the meantime, what is the good of making a scandal? You can make up your mind to it, my boy, I'm free and intend to remain free. Let me pass. When these medical gentlemen arrive, you will make them my excuses for having disturbed them, and if, at all costs, they want to prove how clever they are, they can always busy themselves with you."

Claude listened, speechless with amazement. Suddenly, as M. de Marbois stretched out a hand to open the door, he leaped upon him with such fury, that M. de Marbois, without being able to defend himself, fell backwards. But, hardly had his shoulders touched the floor, than he flung the other off with a jerk, and they began to fight without a word or a cry, arms and legs interlocked, a terrible couple, so closely united that they became one moving mass, now rearing upright, now staggering against the walls that shook under the impact.

Sometimes the violence of a rush, the agony of a bite, separated them: in the darkness they cursed and defied each other and quickly closed up again. After a bite that filled his mouth with the taste of blood, Claude attempted nothing else. With his head held firmly under the arm of M. de Marbois, he tore at the cloth that protected the flesh beneath. Presently, half-suffocated, he ceased his attack. M. de Marbois put a knee on his chest, and sneered, as fresh as though it had all been in play, his strong hands knotted around the thin neck:

"And now?"

Claude panted without replying; M. de Marbois believed him to be at his mercy and loosened his grip.

"Fool!" shouted Claude, raising himself with one bound, and burying the knife, which since yesterday had lain concealed in his pocket, in his neck.

A jet of blood gushed out, splashing his face. Then, every particle of reason that remained in him vanished, and he began to rain blows on the still face, striking with the handle of the knife, with the blade, heaping insults upon it, pinching it with his streaming fingers, seizing the head by the hair and banging it on the floor, and mingling plaintive cries with his yells, as though to offer the dead man to the spirits of the departed.

"Are you content? Now my hands are clean . . . There is no more shadow . . . All is clear, all is beautiful!"

Mère Chagne called from below:

"Are you there, master?"

He did not hear her, and went on raving:

"He would not die, the swine! He held out, but so did I! For twenty years, I have been living for this moment! How well we shall sleep tonight! . . ."

He sat down on the ground, and drew the back of his hand across his brow with an "ouf!" of relief, like a laborer, laying down his burden. His muscles relaxed deliciously, he was growing sleepy, and he sat there like a faithful watch-dog, proud of having defended his house.

Mère Chagne tapped discreetly at the door, and getting no reply, opened it. At first, in spite of the lamp, she could not see anything, and said, as she allowed Dr. Charlier and M. Coutelet to pass:

"I thought as much . . . he has fallen asleep, poor fellow!"

Claude saw the group, and, without rising, asked them to come in.

"Come in, gentlemen, come in! This will interest you, no doubt. Good evening, M. Coutelet."

He rose to his knees and they saw his blood-bespattered face. The apothecary started back.

"Well, M. Coutelet," cried Claude, surprised, "are you offended with me, that you don't shake hands?"

He looked attentively at his hands on which the blood was coagulating in great patches:

"Is that what you object to? . . . My dear sir, I am what I am; you must take what friendship I offer or go away."

Already he was getting up to cast forth the intruders, when his eyes fell on the corpse, and he stopped uncertainly. Blood was everywhere, on the floors, on the walls, on the furniture, the window panes . . . not a thing, not a corner that did not bear its scarlet mark, even his head and body were plastered with it.

"Wretched man!" cried M. Coutelet, while Dr. Charlier, horrified, bent over the dead body, and Mère Chagne took to her heels.

"Well," said Claude, "what's the matter with you all? Don't you know who that is? It is Marbois the murderer, and I have killed him. Since when does one allow a criminal to remain at large? Kill, and thou shalt be killed. Yes, gentlemen, that is my rule. Applaud the chance that has permitted me to punish the guilty on this very spot. His death will appease two souls here. You do not see them; I see them, I hear them. If you only knew what they say to me! Just now, they were laughing; it was the first time I had ever heard them laugh, I their son! A son who never heard the laugh of his parents . . . is such a thing credible?"

Dr. Charlier tried to grasp the arm brandishing the knife. He pulled it away, furiously.

"You are not thinking of arresting me, when the murderer lies there? Why did you not get hold of him thirty years ago? For thirty years the bones of a dead man have lain rotting underground, a poor dead man, whom no one would avenge! But God be thanked, I was watching . . ."

He thought a moment, and shrugged his shoulder indulgently:

"After all you were not supposed to know; if things had not taken *me* into their confidence, I should never have known the secret. The story of this is more wonderful than all your science, M. Coutelet! I can tell it to you. But never repeat it! For, understand, I had but one love on earth, my mother, and it is of her I would speak with you. I would willingly give my hand to prevent the revelation of the slightest thing that might tarnish her memory. But first of all, who is that gentleman listening to me . . . One of your friends? Can I trust him?"

His voice echoed weirdly in the room dimly lighted by Mère Chagne's green-shaded lamp.

"Truth came to me by paths as yet unknown of men. A new sense was offered me, as delicate as sight, as touch, as hearing. Have you ever stopped to think, M. Coutelet, what a human being, gifted with a dog's sense of smell, would be? How many things, hidden from us, would be made clear to him! The sense of which I speak is a thousand-fold richer; it is the sense of the unknown. Who possesses it possesses all things. Thanks to it I roam in the past as through a garden. One wish . . . one concentrated desire, and the present vanishes, I lose the shape of your faces . . . I no longer hear your breathing . . . a wonderful silence surrounds me . . . Hush! I enter the garden of the past . . .

"A date; it is August 13th, 1880. My mother is sitting in her room. She is lost in thought, a book lying on her knees. How sad she looks, and how intently she listens! Yet the house is sleeping, and the wind is so light it hardly rustles the leaves of the trees. Her face contracts, she smiles; again her head droops. M. Deguy enters softly. He leans over her, strokes her hair, and whispers in her ear. She blushes. How quiet everything is, and how full of happiness . . . The night is warm, yet my mother shivers. Then M. Deguy kisses her brow, and withdraws. She remains without moving, beside the window. Ten o'clock . . . eleven o'clock. A shadow crosses the park. It goes its way rapidly, keeping close to the hedges, then once more the door opens, and the shadow appears. Don't you recognize it? It is M. de

Marbois. My mother turns away from him. Her terror amuses him. He speaks:

"'What are you afraid of? He's asleep.'

"She implores him:

"'Do go away!'

"He reassures her:

"'No one can hear us. You must listen to me tonight . . . Do you still refuse yourself? And yet you know quite well that one day, tomorrow perhaps . . . you will be mine . . . You promised me. Then why, at this hour of love, do you turn away from me? Shall we wait until our youth fades . . . or is it that you no longer love me? The other did you say . . . ? An old man who might be your father!'

"She is about to reply. Suddenly they start upright. M. Deguy stands on the threshold, so deathly white that his silvery hair and the skin of his temples seem one. Amazement stuns him at first, then he demands:

"'What are you doing here?'

"He says the words in a terrible voice; then in a pitiful tone:

"'Collette! Collette! is it possible!'

"My mother does not speak. The man sneers. Then M. Deguy seizes a chair and brandishes it. But the man drags it out of his hands, grips hold of him with both arms, and presses. My mother sits there watching all this. She wants to scream . . . Terror gags her and binds her feet. All the horror in the world looks out of her eyes. She hides her face in the palms of her hands, then presses them flat against her sides, as though to hide the sight from every portion of her being. The man still presses. He staggers, gives way under the dead weight dragging on him, and the body of M. Deguy crashes to the ground, there, between the fallen chair, and the book that my mother has dropped.

"Then my mother utters a terrible cry; the man puts his hand over her mouth and threatens:

"'If you say a word, I'm lost, and you with me.'

"She sinks on a couch, fainting. He carries her back to her bed, undresses her . . . naturally . . . to give the impression that she has heard nothing! Then he blows out the lamp, climbs over the balcony, drops into the shrubbery, and runs from lawn to lawn . . . so that he leaves no footmarks . . . scales the wall, and off he goes, away through the countryside."

As he spoke, drops of sweat gathered on his brow, and his voice grew hoarse; he bounded here and there, imitating gestures and facial expressions. It seemed as though he were possessed of a sacred frenzy, that in turn he was the dead man, the unconscious woman, the murderer, and he hurried over his story, hastening to the end, as though the fragile past might melt before his eyes.

"Morning comes. Someone enters, and finds M. Deguy dead in the library, clad in trousers, dressing-gown, nightgown and slippers, like a man getting ready for bed.

"Another date now . . . October 7, 1880! M. le Comte de Marbois marries Mlle. Colette Fagant. Ghastly, isn't it? . . . No indeed, gentlemen, it is nothing. To marry the mistress of the man you have murdered? A very commonplace crime! Who can tell how many others of the same kind have been committed. Like wolves men devour each other. In the one case it is for the sake of a prey; in the other for the sake of a dowry. And, *ma foi*, M. Deguy's fortune is no small matter! Millions, gentlemen, millions! It is well worth strangling a man for. I tell you it is nothing, less than nothing! Before I became a judge have not I, too, desired to kill? You can hardly believe it, and yet . . . ! One day I told a famous physician, and he did not believe me . . . if he had, he would have had me locked up. And that would have been a great pity, as you are going to see.

"For here is the third date, 12 April, 1881; my birthday. Count! from October to April . . . six months. The shadow begins to disperse for you as it did for me, does it not? And to think that no one else thought of making such a calculation! Why, of course you've grasped it; I am the son of M. Deguy. When the murder was committed before her I was in my mother's womb! Yes, my mother, my wretched mother saw that deed! She looked on, a horror-stricken witness at that horrible thing! And that is why I came into the world with a tortured soul, a desire to kill, and these red hands. But now they are white, they will always be white; they had to be washed: I have washed them. Look here, look here! See! . . ."

He stretched his blood-stained hands above his head, moving them about, and uttering little cries of joy.

Suddenly his face paled; he put out a hand, and stammered:

"M. Coutelet? . . . Dr. Charlier?"

Neither of the men answered. Two tears ran down his cheeks, and he said no more. Reason was returning to her place.

A confused babel of voices came from the garden. The farm-people, and soon all the villagers had hastened thither in answer to the cries of Mère Chagne. Lighted lanterns darted about, men and women gesticulated and called one to another. The old people told the young all they knew of the by-gone tragedy, with muttered suspicions and vague threats, but without daring to go right up to the house which had been marked out for the second time by crime.

In the room Claude still wept. Accustomed as he was to such scenes, Dr. Charlier could not control his emotion. M. Coutelet stood with bent head. The murder roused the most terrible doubts within him. Out of the chaos of words and incoherent visions, a logical evocation stood out. A thousand details, hitherto of no importance, struck him with strange force. As he looked back on his conversations with Claude, he discerned the gloomy travail that had been accomplished in his brain.

Had not he himself, unconsciously, guided his research and awakened his suspicions? Wise and prudent man that he was, he had allowed himself to be tricked by a semi-maniac, and he felt upon his old shoulders the weight of a dreadful responsibility.

In a corner, leaning against the wall, Claude stood motionless.

The contrast between his former vehemence and his present attitude was such that the doctor murmured:

"Is he really mad, or is his madness feigned? If I thought there was a particle of truth in all this, I should ask myself whether it was not more a case for an examining magistrate than for me. What is your opinion, Monsieur? You have lived here for forty years. Have you ever heard any of the things to which this young fellow alludes? Is it true that a man was found dead on this spot?"

"It is true," answered M. Coutelet in a very low voice.

"Did you know the mother?"

M. Coutelet was about to reply. Claude stared fixedly at him.

"Yes," murmured the apothecary.

"What sort of a woman was she?"

This time an expression of despair came into Claude's face. His lips moved, he clasped his hands, and held them out in a frantic gesture of appeal.

"She was a delicate, gentle creature," answered M. Coutelet, in a voice that shook with emotion. "Shy and charming, a good, loving, blameless mother . . . She lived . . . I believe . . . a sinless life, and died, as we say here, in a state of grace."

"And so what we have just listened to? . . ."

"Is sheer madness. The crime and the story are the work of a madman . . . ! And look, if we needed any further proof . . ."

Suddenly abandoning his calm attitude, Claude burst into a fit of laughter, then rolled over on the floor, clawing at his face with his hands.

"The rope, quickly!" ordered the doctor.

They seized him, pinioned him in a trice, and laid him on the couch; he still yelled, and struggled to free himself.

Dr. Charlier made sure that the rope was firmly fixed, and said with a sigh:

"It had been brought for the father, and has been used on the son!"

"Alas," said M. Coutelet.

And, as he bent over Claude to free his head which was buried under the cushions, he heard him murmur in a gentle, graceful voice:

"You are a good man, M. Coutelet!"

A PARTIAL LIST OF SNUGGLY BOOKS

LÉON BLOY *The Tarantulas' Parlor and Other Unkind Tales*
S. HENRY BERTHOUD *Misanthropic Tales*
FÉLICIEN CHAMPSAUR *The Latin Orgy*
FÉLICIEN CHAMPSAUR *The Emerald Princess and Other Decadent Fantasies*
BRENDAN CONNELL *Unofficial History of Pi Wei*
QUENTIN S. CRISP *Blue on Blue*
LADY DILKE *The Outcast Spirit and Other Stories*
BERIT ELLINGSEN *Vessel and Solsvart*
EDMOND AND JULES DE GONCOURT *Manette Salomon*
RHYS HUGHES *Cloud Farming in Wales*
JUSTIN ISIS *Divorce Procedures for the Hairdressers of a Metallic and Inconstant Goddess*
VICTOR JOLY *The Unknown Collaborator and Other Legendary Tales*
BERNARD LAZARE *The Mirror of Legends*
JEAN LORRAIN *Errant Vice*
JEAN LORRAIN *Masks in the Tapestry*
JEAN LORRAIN *Nightmares of an Ether-Drinker*
JEAN LORRAIN *The Soul-Drinker and Other Decadent Fantasies*
ARTHUR MACHEN *Ornaments in Jade*
CAMILLE MAUCLAIR *The Frail Soul and Other Stories*
CATULLE MENDÈS *Bluebirds*
LUIS DE MIRANDA *Who Killed the Poet?*
OCTAVE MIRBEAU *The Death of Balzac*
DAMIAN MURPHY *Daughters of Apostasy*
KRISTINE ONG MUSLIM *Butterfly Dream*
YARROW PAISLEY *Mendicant City*
URSULA PFLUG *Down From*
JEAN RICHEPIN *The Bull-Man and the Grasshopper*
DAVID RIX *A Suite in Four Windows*
FREDERICK ROLFE *An Ossuary of the North Lagoon and Other Stories*
JASON ROLFE *An Archive of Human Nonsense*
BRIAN STABLEFORD *Spirits of the Vasty Deep*
BRIAN STABLEFORD (editor) *Decadence and Symbolism: A Showcase Anthology*
JANE DE LA VAUDÈRE *The Demi-Sexes and The Androgynes*
JANE DE LA VAUDÈRE *The Double Star and Other Occult Fantasies*
RENÉE VIVIEN AND HÉLÈNE DE ZUYLEN DE NYEVELT *Faustina and Other Stories*